ANATOMY OF DARKNESS

S. ROIT

SNOWBOOKS

Proudly published by Snowbooks

Copyright © 2015 Sherry Roit
Sherry Roit asserts the moral right to be identified as
the author of this work. All rights reserved.

Snowbooks Ltd
email: info@snowbooks.com
www.snowbooks.com

British Library Cataloguing in Publication Data.

A catalogue record for this book is available
from the British Library.

Paperback / softback ISBN13 9781909679801

First published February 2015

Special thanks to:

Jane Lemmonds – Gandalf
Karen Queeno – who sold her glass eye
Tina Kenney – Broncette
Andrew Hawnt – author, columnist
*Melissa Hopkins – who reads everything I do a bazillion times
and still never hates it.*

I

Air. Thick with sweat. Sweat on a warm day. That of horses and men. Thick with testosterone. Thick with bravery. Fear. Death. It comes to the nose.

It alights on the tongue.

Someone screams.

Laughter. Sadistic laughter.

Joyful, sadistic laughter.

More screaming. Moaning. Begging.

Death rattles.

A mouth opens. Tongue flicks out, tasting the air.

Tastes of blood. Blood spilled, cooling and turning dark, darker. Blood yet to be spilled. Rich. Bright. Pulsing just beneath flesh. Veins standing out from struggle and quickening heart.

Not enough. Covered in it, yet it cools, becomes a lifeless gel too soon. More, find more, laced with terror.

They see a walking nightmare when they see the eyes. Bow or die.

Or just die. This was preferred, wanted, lusted after.

Slowly, die slowly and the blood remains a living thing. Dying slowly, baking in a hot sun. Blood running in tiny rivers over sweaty, hot flesh.

Scent of flesh. Flesh in the sun.

Hundreds. Thousands. What the eyes see is never enough. Bathing in crimson tides, never enough of the feeling. Flooding the land, turning the very sky as red as the vision.

Dying slowly. Pigs rotting in the sun. Rivers of red flow again and again and nothing is felt but the orgiastic pleasure of it. No faces, no names. Nothing but the craving.

God curses. He is cursed in return. This sacrifice belongs not to Him, yet he shares it.

All retreats to the darkness of stone. The darkness of stone and blood. Blood and pain more intimate.

Private.

Not His.

The need.

The need.

THE NEED.

2

Viktor's wild, blind gaze flitted about the bedroom whilst his hands clutched at his chest in an effort to contain the slithering beast that he felt was trying to escape. A beast fashioned by an iron hand in the fires of rage.

And lust.

As focus attempted to return to him in increments, and the small walnut dresser attempted to anchor him to the here and now, he managed to sit up. Or, he found himself sitting up, after taking a few deep breaths that only managed to stop strangling him on the seventh try.

He must have slept longer than he intended. It must have been another dream. Nightmare. He was never certain. He could never remember them. He only remembered how he felt upon waking. Those feelings were too stark to forget.

But it must be nightmares. He'd woken up in these horrible states for years, now. Long enough that he'd surmised there must be at least four different scenarios that he moved through in his sleep. He'd figured it must be so, because there were at least four different waking scenarios. Four distinct reactions, emotions, happenings, one of which he knew the details of from previous bed partners. Yet he still didn't know the half of it and he wouldn't be asking anyone anytime soon, because he'd stopped sleeping with people a long time ago.

Viktor rarely even had sex. In fact, he'd been celibate nearly a year, this time around. Well, except for that one time. That one time a few months ago, and the sex was dark, intense. Thankfully, it wasn't as intense as before the first time he'd tried celibacy.

He certainly hadn't slept over the last time. He hadn't wanted to push his luck.

Viktor barely slept as it was. Catnaps at the most. He'd set alarms to make certain it was never more than forty-five minutes. Forty-five minutes seemed to be the longest he could go before whatever happened to him in his sleep, happened.

Occasionally he didn't hear the alarms, however. Occasionally – more than occasionally – he wondered if he was sleepwalking in broad daylight. He'd black out. Go away. That's what one of his current band-mates had said about it.

You just...go away, sometimes.

Viktor roused himself from the lingering feelings of anger, the feeling that he had somehow been wronged, the feeling that he wanted more, more, and left the bed, noting with some relief that his room wasn't in shambles. Standing before the full-length mirror on the back of the bedroom's door, he stared into his piercing grey eyes. Eyes that attracted people for the way the irises were surrounded in charcoal, the irises themselves clear and icy, though the right one bore a small, reddish-brown spot.

Those eyes could be disconcerting in their intensity. In the way it seemed that they viewed a world others couldn't. In the way they burned so cold, at times.

Those eyes made a slow study of his reflected body. Not the lean arms, torso and legs. Not the broad shoulders or the dark patch at his groin that matched the shoulder-length hair on his head. No, not so much the body itself did those eyes take in.

It was the network of scars on his chest and sides that his gaze absorbed. These were his memories. His sexual liaisons. His armor...and some things he couldn't remember.

The fragile network of lines to the insides of his sinuous thighs, these he knew very well, however.

Dark, intense sex. Blood play. Viktor was fascinated with blood and the drawing of it. In the right hands a thin bit of steel was an exquisite thing.

Then there were the marks on his back that he couldn't currently see, but knew very well where each one was.

Those had nothing to do with sex.

He turned from the mirror and made for the walk-in closet. He had a gig tonight. Mitch, their guitar player, was probably already on his way. Viktor chose black leather pants that fit him like a second-skin and knee high, rubber-soled boots. He thought of their drummer Damona while he deliberated between the wine-colored leather vest and the long sleeved, black mesh pull over.

Damona liked it when he mixed colors, but she also liked it when he imitated a shadow in black on black.

He chose the mesh shirt. His scars would show, some of them, but Viktor didn't care about that. He didn't hide his scars. They served as a warning, a signal.

You might want to stay away from me.

You might not care to hear the back-story on some of these scars.

His thoughts turned once more to the redhead he'd been making music with for two years, now. He'd love to make several other kinds of music with her, but he dared not, had never dared to, even though he was certain that she wanted him, too.

He didn't dare, because he didn't want a one-night-stand with Damona. He really liked her. More than liked her, and a one-night-stand was all it could ever be, which wasn't enough by far.

Besides. Even one-night-stands were dangerous.

After dressing, he slipped a long bladed, serrated edged knife into his left boot. He probably shouldn't carry the knife – he knew that he shouldn't carry the knife, given his...*condi-*

tion, whatever it was, but he wasn't able to resist, unlike with the sex. It was difficult enough resisting the sex, but both? He didn't have the will to resist both, as strong-willed as he was.

The long cold steel seduced him. The honed edges made him hard. The sound of it whisper snicking into his boot was *orgasmic*.

He didn't know why. Like many things about Viktor, it was what it was. Something he had to accept about himself, or drive himself insane wondering about.

Viktor chose to keep whatever sanity he might actually possess, and stopped questioning a couple of years ago. It was what it was and it was always good to have protection. He'd learned very well, the value of protection.

Yes, he'd learned, but more than this, in his heart of hearts, in the dark squishy folds of his gut, he knew that Death was stalking him. Old age wouldn't be his killer. His death was going to be bloody. A bloody, horrible death.

Viktor had made peace with that, for the most part. He'd known for a long time, because even his mother had told him this when he was a child. He could no longer look to her for guidance, however. Not for support.

Death had already claimed his mother.

He surveyed himself in the mirror once more. Satisfied, he grabbed his bass and made his way out of the tiny, rented loft, to go sit outside on the front steps and wait for Mitch.

3

They exited the midnight blue van and went around the back of it to grab their gear, the gravel of the lot crunching beneath their feet.

"Looks like it'll be another good crowd, tonight," Mitch said. "They're already lining up." As he said this, his eyes moved over the shamble of a building, which needed a major facelift. Its gutters sagged, the door tilted on its hinges, and what was left of the paint was peeling – for starters. The inside wasn't much better, just a rattrap of a place in nowhere-ville, but it held many people which meant more money when it was full.

Viktor paused to look at his blond-haired companion. "We've gained a reputation. They remember us from the last time we came through."

Mitch's smile was quick to come, as many of them were, and it was a good smile, Mitch's smile. "*Satan's Whore* rocks the house, dude." He high-fived the taller man, then reached for his guitar case. "'Course, mostly they're into you."

"Don't sell yourself short," Viktor replied. "You're a good looking man who plays a sweet guitar solo."

"Yeah, but singers always get most of the attention. It's just the way it is."

Viktor's eyes crinkled with his smile as he pulled his bass from the back of the van. "Even so, you're being falsely modest. Women flock to you after a gig."

"You, too, but you're so damned creepy, only the most determined, or stalker-ish, stick around." Mitch set down his guitar case, his study of Viktor while he did so, rather indiscreet.

Viktor looked him dead in the eyes. "Creepy?"

"You know what I mean, bro'. You're so intense and stand-offish." Mitch had teased Viktor about this before, perhaps not so directly, but he had. Only now he wasn't quite teasing.

The taller man, easily 6'4" to the blond's 5'11", gave off a light shrug. "I do know. It's better that way. They need to be brave if they're going to hang around me."

"So you've said before."

"So you've witnessed, Mitch."

This statement silenced the young guitarist for a moment, two. He had witnessed some things no one should witness, especially when these things involved a friend. Someone you thought well of, someone you really liked, yet couldn't comprehend, not fully. Nor could you comprehend what you'd seen.

Mitch had never uttered a word about it to the wrong people. Not a word to anyone, in fact. He wasn't sure why. Probably he should have, still should, but he wouldn't. He wasn't a snitch. He didn't have a perfect past himself, and he knew that Viktor would never rat him out. Still, he thought that he should probably be afraid of Viktor, but he'd never actually *been* afraid of Viktor. And really, it was just the one time, only once, that Viktor had done something that truly freaked him out, and it wasn't all Viktor's fault. It wasn't even so much what Viktor had done, but *how* he'd done it that had so shocked Mitch.

Viktor hadn't done anything like that again, though. Not that Mitch knew of, anyway. Everyone makes mistakes; that's what he told himself. Everyone deserves a second chance.

Sure, the bass-player-slash-lead-singer was possibly a bit crazy in some way that Mitch didn't understand, but Viktor was his friend. Viktor had always stood up for him, stood by his side, and Viktor had never been anything but nice to him, if a little distant at times.

Distant? Hell, they'd been on the road on and off together for nearly three years, now, and Viktor had never bunked with Damona and him, and this was especially odd to Mitch, because he was certain Viktor wanted to nail Damona. Hell, Viktor wouldn't even sleep in the van when they were on an extended tour. He always insisted on driving.

The truth was Mitch worried about Viktor, even though he appeared well adjusted in many other ways. Yet the blond couldn't shake the feeling that his brunet sidekick needed some kind of help, whether Viktor thought so, or not.

But he played a mean bass and sang a haunting melody that never left your memory or your senses. Mitch had never heard anyone sing the way that Viktor sang. Had never been moved the way Viktor could move him. As if his soul bled through the songs. As if it was trying to escape and free all of the other prisoners along the way.

"Yeah," Mitch said at last, to no one in particular. He then felt a twinge of guilt when he realized that Viktor had already gotten most of the gear out of the van while he'd been standing there sifting through thoughts. Something Viktor always appeared to understand.

"Let's get in there and set up," Viktor said. "Damona would probably like some help."

Mitch contemplated, as he often did, that maybe he was drawn to the mystery of Viktor as much as to Viktor himself. To the darkness, and the source of it, whatever it was.

"Probably would." Mitch lifted his guitar in one hand, gig bag in the other, and fell into Viktor's long-legged pace as best he could.

**

The copper-haired woman behind the drums tamped out an easy beat, her porcelain arms reflecting the red, blue, green, and yellow of the stage lights. An easy yet intense beat to match the dissonant guitar chords and the soft, pulsing bass line.

It was the mellifluous tones of the singer that held most rapt, however.

Speak me gently
Your ears burn my voice
Speak me now
Without a catch in...your throat

Viktor's lyrics cut a pleading, sensuous line through the nicotine-staled air; the product of carpet never replaced and walls not washed since indoor smoking became illegal, made somehow worse in the aging process.

Sing me low
I could sink way down
Pick me up
Before my heart hits...the ground

Years old cigarettes and fresh sweat, which glistened off faces held in rapt attention, faces uplifted, lips mouthing words some didn't even know. It was always like that when Viktor sang, always as if he wove a spell, cast a magic web over the crowd and brought them into his surreal world, the strands made of dream, smoke, need, want, lust and loss. A world made of rapture, pain and frustration.

Those who listened, who felt the draw, couldn't adequately explain what the draw was, no more than Viktor could explain where the music came from. It just was, and it was good, and it had always been so.

Unlock the pages
Of ages long ago
Smell the ashes
Of words to forego
Soft my heart... listens to your walk
Speaking now
Please... don't go...

As the song faded, Viktor whisper singing the final words...

Kiss me softly and look at me

A roomful of people were his to command, to mold, to manipulate...

Kiss me softly, just breathe.

And when the last note rang out, echoing through the dismal, dingy room, the spell remained, everyone in suspended animation. This was not lost on Viktor. It was a glorious exchange, the energy given, the energy returned, as if they had all become one giant vampire, feeding, feeding.

It wasn't lost on Mitch, either, who generally ended up breaking the spell with a *whoop* and the usual band-to-bar-crowd banter, nonetheless. Tonight was no different.

The performers wandered off stage, preparing to pack up their gear. Preparing in this instance meant having as many free drinks as possible before the bar shut down. At least for Mitch it did. Viktor didn't usually drink a vast amount, and even when he did, he didn't appear to get drunk; something Mitch was infinitely jealous of. As for Damona, she was generally content to hang with Viktor and basically do whatever he did.

"Great set, man," someone said as Viktor reached the bar. Though the man spoke to Viktor his eyes devoured Damona, who stood close to her band-mate, her Monroe-like curves swathed in pink and black latex.

"Thank you," said Viktor, and then to the bartender, "Vodka Collins and a Chivas, please." He glanced at his drummer. She was nearly a foot shorter than he was, but she remedied this with all manner of sexy high heels, like the black thigh-high boots she was currently wearing. Onstage she went barefoot. Also quite sexy, what with the blood-red polish she always used on her nails. It was vivid like a homicide against her pale skin.

Viktor grabbed a stool and sat, ready to see more of her thighs when she opted to sit beside him.

"You been hitting the skins a long time?" the stranger asked, his words now directed at Damona.

"A while," she said, while she took a stool between the ginger-haired man and Viktor, just as predicted in Viktor's mind.

The bar-patron's eyes moved between the two musicians. "Maybe you could teach me a few things." He smiled at Damona in a way that attempted to be suave, but failed.

Viktor returned his attention to the stranger. "Hit some *skins*, perhaps?" His gaze pressed down on the other man.

A shiver raced along the ginger-man's spine. "Sorry, dude," he said, and made a swift retreat. Damona, unconcerned, placed a possessive hand on Viktor's arm and Viktor swung his gaze to her.

"I'm sorry," he said. He wasn't certain what had come over him. He wasn't quite certain why the man had stumbled over himself in his effort to get away. Had he sounded jealous?

Yes, he wanted Damona, but he couldn't have her. She wasn't his. Generally he wasn't jealous or possessive. He knew it wasn't right. She hadn't needed protecting, either. Had he sounded threatening? There was no point in asking Damona; she always said that things were cool.

"Go on and find him," Viktor said, still unsure of what he'd done, but convinced that he should make amends. "He might be fun."

Damona's hand gave his arm a little squeeze before she reached for her Vodka Collins. "I doubt it." Her lips pursed around the small straw as she drank, in a way that Viktor found unbearably seductive. "I'm content here."

She often said such things. She was content to follow him around, to sit with him no matter his mood, to….What, content to wait for him to come around?

It wasn't right, as much as it touched him at times. As much as it pleased him. She gave off a heavy submissive vibe, too, which turned him on.

It was also another reason he couldn't have her. Her vibe sometimes did strange things to him. Either that, or when he was in certain strange moods, her vibe was far too tempting. He hadn't answered the chicken-or-egg question, yet. He just knew that unsettling things percolated through his system when he was with her. Things he couldn't describe, and things he shouldn't describe.

He tossed back his Chivas and ordered another, satisfied to let things stand in silence, for now. Yet another wonderful thing about Damona. She didn't ask him many questions.

4

Coldness. Stone. Darkness. Stone.

Sometimes a little light. Tarnished, filtered light, dingy light.

Youth. Youth on the stone cold stone floor. A rat scurrying by.

Voices. Older, masculine.

Dragged out.

Stripped again. Smell of leather.
Stinging. Burning, stinging.

Cries. Crying out.

But no begging.

The youth had begun this time being properly afraid of torture. Perhaps not as much as the others, stubborn and proud as he was, but afraid, as he was meant to be.

Time passing. Fear begins to leave.

Fear becomes defiance.

Flesh being spliced. Warm trickles of life fluid.

Defiance grows, fear's last finger-hold slipping away.

It becomes a game.

Stripped. Sweet smell of leather.

Sting. Sweet, sweet burning sting.

More. Want more.

Hatred's poison blooms larger and larger with every close-fisted hit, every strike of wood, but with it also comes desire.

Desire for the other tortures.

Leather is sweet, so sweet, but metal is better.

Flesh being spliced. The heady scent of blood.

They see the arousal, it cannot be hidden, the body so bare.

Some begin to fear. Words, whispered words. The Devil has him, the Devil has him.

Some think madness. Madness for many still given as being of the Devil.

One of the soldiers of God's seed, of the Devil?

Some think... interesting.

Kill the Devil's spawn!
Set him free.
Kill him!
Set him free.
He could be an asset.

Kill him!

He will be set free. One with this strong of will, shall be set free. He was but a pawn, anyway.

But first.

Discussions. Darkly informative discussions on the anatomy of the human body. On the effectiveness of certain methods.
A youth takes it all in and adds secret, mental notes.

Hatred grows.
A Father and Brother assassinated.
Brother tortured, buried alive.
They spared no detail.

Revenge.
Desire, burning hot.

Revenge.

Desire, burning hot, unclean.
Pain.

A stone cold floor. The last night. A stone cold floor.

"Give me the power and I will give You Blood."
"You will kill for your own pleasure."
"I will share the pleasure with You. Stand by me when I avenge and all Sacrifice will be in Your name. Do not betray me! They died for You!"
"They died in my cause."
"Yes! Yes! Your cause. Defending Your cause. Give me the power!"
"You shall have my power, but this power will pervert you further and further. Do you still ask it of me?"
"Yes! I ask You, not the Devil!"
"Kneel."

Kneeling. Hard stone on bare knees. Covenant made.

Dragged out.

One last torture, for old time's sake. Stripped.

Cold metal.
Small rivers of blood.
Ecstasy.

Thrown out of the prison, nearly thrown as if it cannot be rid of him fast enough. Vomited out.

A sadistic smile forms on a far too youthful face. A once more innocent face.

There will be other Blood soon, so very soon.

5

Viktor woke. His heart beat faster and faster. His sheets were damp with sweat, but not from fear. After a moment he rose and went to the bathroom to view himself in the mirror. He often needed to look into the mirror after a nightmare, if only to see that he was still…Viktor.

He studied his nude reflection. Still scarred, and part of him stood at attention. The scars brought a smile to Viktor's lips, a smile that was dark and heated, just as his gaze was dark, heated.

Desire rose in a fiery flush over his skin. It flamed low in his body, in his belly, in his groin, and burned in his brain.

He lifted a short, steel blade that his hand easily found on the bathroom counter. His smile shifted, becoming sadistic and determined. The blade parted skin close, so very close, to his right nipple. His moan was deep, rising in a sigh from the bowels of a bottomless well.

Grey eyes watched the rivulets of red appear and tracked their downward dance over winter-paled flesh.

He smeared it with his free hand, running his fingers through the sticky droplets, which he then brought to his lips. Like a cat, he licked at his fingers, his palm, licked until no trace of his life force was left.

He then grasped the length of his penis and began to stroke. The blade clattered on the floor.

It wasn't enough. It would never be enough.

Grey eyes stared, watched the stroking. Watched the fresh beads of blood blossom on his chest from the crescent shaped cut.

Harder. Faster. Harder. New droplets bloomed.

He stayed his hand. It wasn't enough. It required a partner. Someone else's hand. Someone else to hold the blade. Someone else for him to cut while he was buried deep inside of them. Someone else to cut him while he was hilted inside of them.

Or they were buried in him. Either gender was fine with Viktor. For Viktor pleasure was pleasure, people were people. Gender was only visible.

He needed someone else to lick the blood with laconic sweeps of a somewhat rough tongue. Someone who wasn't afraid to bite. Someone who wasn't squeamish, someone who wouldn't call him a sick freak and make him angry. Viktor wasn't pleasant company when he was angry, not pleasant company at all.

Viktor snapped from his reflected reverie and considered dressing. Instead, he sat on the edge of his bed while something of himself returned – or at least tried to return.

The band was in Europe, now. Just outside of Paris, France. Mitch had finally gotten a passport after months and months of searching for a copy of his birth certificate; a search that had involved tracking down his absent mother. Mitch hadn't even known where he was born. Damona and Viktor were born in Europe, and so had less trouble with such things, though Viktor wasn't always welcomed with open arms. The way he travelled in the past, the people he associated with, and the way he looked: these things didn't help him.

Viktor was of Romani stock. A gypsy, as some called them, though the Rom didn't always like this word. Not that it mattered much to Viktor anymore, because even most of the Rom shunned him, and had for some long time. He didn't care what people called him as long as they left him alone.

His gaze moved around the cramped hotel room whilst his thoughts turned to events past; to a mysterious man he'd met in Paris. Down in the catacombs is where Viktor had had the pleasure. Or, not pleasure, depending on the point of view.

He'd been taken there by some other mysterious people, people Viktor had come upon in Pigalle. Viktor had been in a dangerous mood that night, a mood brought on by one of his night terrors. He'd hit the streets of Paris as soon as he'd dressed. A dangerous mood, but it wasn't precisely that he was dangerous to someone else.

Viktor had been chasing Death, because he was tired of being followed. He'd found it, too. The four that escorted him to the catacombs were intent on slicing him up, and not in the way that he preferred, though it had seemed clear at the time that his hosts would find it quite pleasurable. They'd tied him down and pulled out knives, one of which was exactly the same as the one he always carried in his left boot, now.

A souvenir courtesy of his Savior.

This savior didn't come with wings, hallelujahs, or even golden, heavenly light. No choirs, no harps and no halos. On the contrary; salvation came as a swift dark shadow with sparks of light glancing off cold steel, and at the center of this mysterious whirlwind flew long jet strands and a flash of white.

Viktor stood up and walked to his duffel, contemplating attire for the evening. He thought that he might remember where his Savior had taken him that night. The place where he'd woken up. He would certainly never forget the look of the place. For a time, he'd been convinced that he'd been taken to Japan.

He might be able to find that house. He felt that it wasn't far, though he was uncertain as to why. There *was* a theory in his mind.

It was the man. He was connected in some way to the man. The one who told him that Death chose its own time and place, and that those tunnels had not been the time, or the place. It was the man who told him that Death in the catacombs wasn't the same Death who'd been stalking him.

He might be able to find the sleek stranger who never answered when Viktor had asked what imitation of Death those four people had planned to give him.

He'd known. Viktor had known that those people were murderous. He'd felt the hair on his arms lift away from his skin. He'd seen the look in their eyes. The hunger. He'd known they would try to kill him. It's why he allowed himself to be captured.

His mother would've said that they were demons.

His Savior's presence did the same to his body hair. His Savior had had a similar glint in his eyes. But it wasn't directed at Viktor. Viktor wanted to be close to that presence, again. A strong, dark, yet noble presence. His Savior seemed like someone that Viktor couldn't hurt. He had given the appearance of understanding Viktor in some way that no one else did, or ever would.

This was saying a lot, as Viktor didn't always understand *himself*.

It had been too brief, his stay with his Savior. But he hadn't forgotten him. Never would. It had been too long since Viktor had been in France. Since he'd woken up in California, never knowing how he'd gotten there, though he was certain that his Savior had something to do with it – and Viktor did consider the man his Savior even though he'd snatched him from the icy hands of Death. Viktor hadn't exactly wanted to die, he'd just wanted to spit in Death's face and put up a fight. At least, that's what he'd decided after waking up alive, that fateful night.

Resolved, since they had no gig this evening and Mitch and Damona were, or should be, asleep in their own room on another floor, Viktor dressed. Knife in boot, he left the hotel, following his sixth sense, as some would've called it. It wasn't as if he could look the man up in some directory. The Savior had given Viktor a name, but only one. A single name, just as Viktor had only one name.

This had been another source of trouble for Viktor the moment he was born. Another reason he was considered an outcast. No Father had been present to name him. His mother was shunned for having a bastard child – amongst other things.

His thoughts turned back to the stranger. If he found the Asian, maybe he could convince the man to bleed him; Viktor was yet in a dangerously lusty mood, and he remembered well how drawn to blood the other man had seemed to be. The would-be killers had already cut him when the stranger arrived, and Viktor had a vivid, fevered memory of his Savior licking his wounds. He was certain it hadn't been just a dream. Fairly certain.

He'd find out once and for all when he found the man who called himself Kar.

**

Mitch rolled onto his left side and stared at Damona, who was absorbed in one of her comic books. Which one, he couldn't tell. The only light on in the room was a tiny, portable reading light she'd purchased a few towns ago in the States.

Mitch couldn't sleep. He was restless, uneasy. Or rather, his mind was. The second he'd gotten his passport, Viktor had insisted that they get to France, and Mitch hadn't heard Viktor insist on anything, before this. Except that he was dangerous. Viktor was *very* certain of that, apparently.

Mitch couldn't stop wondering what the deal was with France. Couldn't stop feeling…suspicious. About what, he wasn't sure.

Viktor had sprung for the plane tickets and hotels, so far. That in itself wasn't completely off-the-wall. He'd paid for rooms before, and Viktor often rented a small flat (exclusively for himself) when they were going to be in an area for a while. Two weeks could be a while, where Viktor was concerned. He always seemed to have money, just enough money. It wasn't as if he spent much. Just strings for his bass and other necessities. He rarely even bought clothes.

And he sharpened his knives himself.

Mitch sat up a little, now dwelling on steel, Viktor's steel, and in particular, the crazy knife he knew was always tucked away in Viktor's boot.

Viktor *always* wore boots.

Unbeknownst to Mitch, a tremble disturbed his limbs when he thought of what he'd seen Viktor's knife do. It was followed by a shiver when he realized how he'd phrased it in his head. What he'd seen his *knife* do.

The tremble didn't get past Damona, who had at that moment, looked over at her roommate.

"Something is wrong? You cold?" she asked, but she didn't think it was a chill.

"Huh?" Mitch blinked and refocused on her face. He'd been staring through her a second before. "Oh. No. I'm good."

She studied him, studied his blue eyes. She debated her next question. Damona wasn't one to pry. She was unobtrusive to the point of appearing unsympathetic and uncaring, sometimes even to the people who knew her. Only Viktor knew better one hundred percent of the time.

Decision reached, she said, "You're thinking about Viktor." Not a question, a statement. Mitch could confirm, deny, or ignore her, as he pleased.

He opted for a shrug.

Damona dropped her eyes to the black and white pages resting on her legs, where *Tank Girl's* mouth was flirting with disaster yet again.

"Though…he has been secretive, lately," Mitch said. "Don't you think?"

This elicited a wry laugh and amused look from Damona. "Compared to what? A mute spy?"

Mitch rolled his eyes. "What I mean is – I mean…" He wasn't certain what he meant, now.

Damona continued to hand him a tranquil stare.

Mitch scooted across his bed and got up. "I'm gonna see if Viktor's up." He headed towards the door. "Stop pestering you with nonsense."

"He's always awake. Why not see if he wants a drink? I still have some vodka."

Mitch glanced across his shoulder at her, but she had already returned to the disjointed adventures of *Tank Girl*.

So he said, "Back soon," and left.

He was back two minutes later.

Damona tore her eyes away from mutant kangaroos when she felt something off in the vibe.

"He's not there," Mitch said.

"Don't look so troubled, pet," Damona purred. "He does it all the time. Leaves, goes for a walk. Always comes back."

"Yeah, but…" Mitch ran a hand through his hair. But what? He didn't know why he was feeling so anxious about the bass player, not really. "Just a weird feeling."

The redhead tossed her comic on the nightstand and gave him a hard look. "You're the one being weird."

Mitch helped himself to an edge of her bed, close to her right arm. "We don't know much about him, you realize. Not really."

Damona arched a brow and let go with a small snort. "You just now understand this?" She lifted and dropped a shoulder.

"What is your point, anyway? Who knows anyone, really?" She poked at him with a finger. "I don't know you."

He stretched out beside her, head by her feet, and poked her leg in return. "What's to know? Foster homes, juvie-hall, finally escaped. Your regular aimless surfer from L.A. trying to make good." He paused, a bit of mischief in his eyes. "Or at least, make it better. That story's a dime a dozen."

And it was, as far as Mitch was concerned. Beach bunny gets pregnant. Beach bum stays long enough to do it twice, and then leaves. Beach bunny turns into beach junkie, dumps kids, kids fend for selves and are eventually separated.

"I'm just another movie of the week," Mitch added, when Damona said nothing. "And what about you? You're from Croatia, wherever that is, and that's about all I know."

Damona's lips quirked at their corners. "Just another sob story that Hollywood loves to fuck up with a happy ending," she said, her face smoothing, giving nothing away. "Conflict, parents killed, refugees, girl eventually makes great escape to America and is given keys to city by President, at her wedding to rich businessman with big heart and big cock. Right?"

They both laughed, Mitch the loudest. He placed a hand on her shin, the touch brotherly. Sure, when he'd met her, he'd wanted to nail her, too, but he'd soon discovered that one: she wasn't into him, and two: he probably wouldn't know what to do with her anyway, if he was being honest with himself. He had a feeling that she was too much wildcat for even the stoutest street kid. Though around Vik, she mellowed.

"Well. That's why we all get along, right?" Mitch said. "Three outcasts form rag-tag group, bond musketeer-like, for the commonality of their secrets."

"Then one shows himself to be a psycho-killer," Damona said, a smile forming.

"You can't lay off the horror flicks, can you?" Mitch replied with a wink – though he thought of Viktor, again.

She shook her head. "If we're going to be predictable, then go for it. What do you say…tongue in your cheek."

Mitch nodded, but said nothing. After staring at him a moment longer, Damona reached for her comic and opened it to the beginning. She had an idea what Mitch was thinking, but a nice thing about Damona was that she didn't ask many questions.

She didn't have to.

6

Viktor stood in the embrace of a tree's moon-induced shadow, just across the road from a large iron gate, which guarded a long drive. It led to a home he knew resembled no other for miles and miles.

He didn't quite remember his journey. He didn't know how long it had taken, or precisely how he'd arrived at the spot he now stood. But he could close his eyes and envision the house, which was well off the road and shrouded in darkness. He could see it in his mind's eye, in his memory. He could see the *Shoin-zukuri* style abode, the type warriors favored, and the Koi pond close to the front doors. He could even see the fish swimming, flashes of white, black and orange.

He could see the interior of the house in greater detail. It had been somewhat awe-inspiring and he'd viewed it for a longer period, back then. The main room contained a sunken alcove, staggered shelves on the walls, and built-in desks. Aisles split off from each side of the room, and down those aisles were rooms separated by ornate, hand-painted *fusuma* sliding doors, and all of the floors were overlaid in *tatami*: rice straw mats covered in woven soft rush straw, with elegant brocade edging. It was often reserved for the wealthy, or greatly honored, which sometimes was one and the same.

He could picture the simple, elegant tearoom at the end of one aisle, with its low, long table and doors that opened to a path through a garden that was worthy of Feudal Japan.

He could see the simple room with traditional bed mat he'd convalesced on, which hadn't taken long. Viktor always wondered why, since he'd had grievous injuries...or so he'd thought, anyway.

He could nearly conjure the taste of the herbal tea his Savior had made him drink. Potent. Warm all the way down his throat. Even through his limbs.

His mouth watered and he shivered with the memory.

What was it about this man, besides the fact that it seemed he was quite out of place in France?

Perhaps not just in France, but in this time period.

Viktor took a quick survey of his surroundings. How far was he from the hotel?

Not having an immediate answer, he chose to cross the road, coming to a stop at the gate. He studied the simple vertical bars, which were dissected here and there by other bits of iron. From his vantage point under the tree, a face had stared back at him. A face in black metal, that of a dragon. Up close, it was merely a break in the normal pattern of the bars.

The finials were quite lethal, however.

Viktor pressed the button on the intercom and waited.

Nothing happened.

He pressed it again. He'd come this far, after all, so he might as well get on with it, no need to be shy. He was unsurprised when once again, nothing happened. He hadn't even truly expected to find the house – not on the first try, anyway. Although, since he had found it, he wouldn't have been stunned to hear the Asian's voice animate the speaker.

When that *still* didn't happen, Viktor contemplated casing the area to look for a way in. The thought was brief, there and gone. He was certain that it couldn't be that simple. That even if there were an opening in the perimeter, something – or someone – would be waiting to greet him with resistance.

Viktor wasn't afraid. The idea that someone was guarding the place wasn't what stopped him. It had to do with respect. As much as he wanted to be on the other side of the high walls, as drawn to the house as he was, he knew that he should wait for an invitation. It was the right thing to do. He needed to wait for his Savior. Breaking in would break something in their…

He couldn't call it a relationship. He hadn't seen or heard from the man since he woke up in L.A. nearly three years ago.

A trust, there was a tenuous trust. At least, on Viktor's part there was. Kar would never trust him if he broke in, and he'd never respect Viktor in return.

Viktor very much wanted the man's respect.

The sound of an engine drawing near pulled Viktor from his thoughts. He turned when he discerned that the vehicle had slowed, and then come to a stop behind him on the road.

As soon as his gaze landed on the dark sedan, someone in the passenger side yelled at him in French.

"Forget your key, imbecile?"

This was followed by the sound of immature, male laughter. More than one male.

"Or maybe your girl kicked you out."

"And her lover is inside now. Way inside!"

Viktor made with a slight tilt of his head as he surveyed those in the car. He'd counted three voices, and his eyes confirmed that there were three silhouettes. He refrained from speech. No matter where you were in the world, guys like this, that's what they wanted: to get their kicks getting a rise out of a stranger, a tourist. Maybe more than a rise. Say the wrong thing, according to them, and it was reason enough to attack.

"Did she steal your tongue, too?" the back seat passenger said.

"How about your wallet?" the driver said.

Viktor's head tilted the other way. So they thought they might rob him, too. He decided that they'd go away empty-handed if they tried. He then had a sudden flash in his mind's eye, that of a dragonfly. His head tilted back the other way yet again while he contemplated this.

"Hey, asshole!" the front seat passenger yelled. "You too good to speak to us or something?"

"I think he's more fucked up than us!" back-seat-man said. "Look at him, his head won't stay on straight."

"He's a retard," front-seat-man said.

They were brash, somewhat drunk, and perhaps a bit high; they thought fucking with the stranger was fun. Viktor might have walked away and let it go, but he felt they'd follow, anyway. He couldn't climb the fence, either. But that didn't matter. The fun was quite swiftly turning serious, as the one who'd just spoken exited the car, followed by the man – boy, really, he could scarce be 19 – in the back seat. Viktor wasn't about to back down, now. He wasn't the type.

Apparently, not speaking was offense enough for them. Viktor continued to stand in silence, even as they kept taunting him, even as the driver began to open his door. Even as they puffed out their chests and threatened him.

Viktor didn't move or flinch, though his brain was over-active with its own chemical reaction.

The young men took this as a sign of weakness, of being too scared to speak or run, on Viktor's part. They couldn't see, in the gathering darkness, the way the piercing grey eyes looking back at them began to glaze over, become glassy. How they shifted and turned dark with malice.

They had intended to ruffle the stranger, maybe roll him for a few bucks and leave him, for the most part, unharmed. That was, until he at last spoke four words.

"What? What kind of screwed up language is that, fucker?" the driver said in response.

But it was too late for questions. In a blinding instant, their prey had become hunter, his malevolent smile briefly reflected in cold steel.

**

Mitch leaned back against the hotel building's south corner and took a slow drag off his cigarette. The cloying scent of clove filled the air around him. It was one of Viktor's hand-rolled creations. Viktor never smoked regular tobacco, always cloves.

It was the scent of a clove cigarette that had drawn Mitch to Viktor nearly three years ago. He'd followed the sweet trail of burning clove and found the tall, dark man sitting on an old, burned-out Buick, just off Hollywood Boulevard. He'd immediately known there was something different about Viktor. Because of this, it had been easier to trust the gypsy. That and the immediate sense that Viktor had secrets, and someone with secrets was less likely to spill someone else's.

Mitch didn't trust anyone until he met the gypsy. *Excuse me, the Rom. Is Roma plural?* Viktor was so tight-lipped that even Mitch knew little about him, though he'd known him longer than Damona. What he *did* know was pretty heavy. Such things made up for small talk, and so he hadn't sweated it much over the time they'd known each other.

Not until more recently.

Mitch took another drag off his clove, letting the smoke out in a lazy, swirling puff around his face. Right now, he was wishing that Viktor wasn't so secretive. It was about an hour before sunrise and the leader of their little band was still absent. Mitch knew, because he'd been restless, and knocked on Vik's door several times during the night.

Damona, on the other hand, was out cold. She could sleep anywhere, during anything.

The guitarist dropped the remaining stub of his smoke and murdered it beneath a heel. *Viktor's a big boy. He can take care of himself.*

Repeat it enough times maybe you'll believe it.

He ran his hands through his short, shaggy blond hair and sighed. He wasn't only worried about Viktor. He worried for anyone who might run *into* Viktor. His bass player had come across as edgy earlier in the day. More intense than usual.

The twenty-five-year-old's thoughts drifted to a summer night almost two years ago. A cool, edge-of-the-desert sort of night in Nevada, when one of two men got all up in Viktor's face, calling him a dirty hippie. The nicest term of the night, but as inaccurate as the rest.

Mitch closed his eyes with the memory, letting it play out against his eyelids. His new friend, who made beautiful hand-beaded belts, bracelets and necklaces, had remained rather calm; that is, until the less vocal of the two strangers decided to speak up, and made fun of the necklace Viktor was wearing. The stranger had then made a grab for it.

That's when Viktor had lost it, yes. When the stranger had reached for his necklace. Mitch had rationalized it several times, since then. The necklace, which Viktor wore to this day, was special. Full of charms; a gift from his dead mother. Mitch could understand not wanting to lose it. And sure, Vik took that stuff very, very seriously.

Still.

Mitch wasn't certain that possibly losing a necklace deserved such a violent reaction, even if the charms were literally magical. Which he doubted. Most of the time.

So he reasoned that Viktor might've thought the man was reaching for him, not the beads. That Viktor felt threatened, maybe thinking the guy was going to punch him. Maybe he thought the man had a weapon. Mitch wasn't certain. It had happened rather fast. The guy might've come at him with a closed fist. He might've done something that only Viktor saw.

It might've been a look in the other man's eyes. Viktor was good at seeing things in other people's eyes. He was good at sensing things about people. He was sometimes even good about knowing the future, in a manner of speaking. Mitch hadn't quite known that at the time, hadn't come to believe in it yet, but he'd been convinced later, and it was immediately applied in his brain as an explanation for the incident.

Mitch pulled away from the wall and rubbed his face. The problem with his theory of Viktor having sensed imminent danger to his person was that Viktor hadn't seemed to know what he'd done after he did it, or why. Hell, he hadn't seemed to know what he was doing *while* he did it.

No. That wasn't entirely accurate.

His movements spoke of cold, surgical precision. Cold; the look in Viktor's eyes, the smile, all cold.

But it didn't seem like Viktor.

Viktor hadn't looked like the Viktor he'd known up until that point, and when it was over, Mitch had had to drag him away, convince him that they needed to get the hell out of there. Should he have called the cops? Maybe. But he hadn't, and he didn't regret it, not really.

He just wished Viktor would trust him enough to tell him if there had been any other incidents like that. To unburden himself, if he needed to. Ask for help, maybe.

As Mitch headed back inside, thinking he'd find coffee, since sleep wasn't coming, he reminded himself that Viktor might not remember similar face-offs, anyway.

If there were any others. Mitch hated to admit it to himself, but he thought it was likely.

7

Viktor sat up with a start. He looked around, wondering how he'd ended up on his ass in front of the dragon-faced gate.

Wasn't I just being harassed by three French wanna-be thugs?

He scanned the area again as he got to his feet, feeling the familiar press of steel in his boot when he did. Familiar, but for a moment, surprising. He couldn't explain to himself why it seemed, just for that moment, that it shouldn't be there.

He turned and looked through the iron bars. The drive wasn't as darkened as he last remembered. He lifted his face to the sky.

"Dawn isn't far." *How is this so?*

He turned and looked back towards the tree he'd been standing under before.

I...went away?

He looked down at his hands: clean. His boots: clean. He surveyed the ground around his feet.

Clean.

Once more, he turned and stared down the long drive in the direction of the house. On and on he stared, his patience nearly infinite. But nothing stirred.

Calm, if somewhat confused, and disappointed if somewhat hopeful, he walked out into the road and in the direction that he remembered the town and his hotel, to be. A few steps down the road, something caught his eye.

A dark blue sedan was off the road, and in another patch of trees. A sedan that Viktor thought he recognized. After walking around it, he was positive that he recognized it; but there were no thugs. There was no one at all, and more curiously, when Viktor looked through the driver side window, he saw the keys in the ignition.

Suspicious of gift horses, he contemplated his position. He was sure it would take quite a while to walk back to town. He felt that it was rather far. He didn't mind walking, but Damona and Mitch might worry if they found him gone. The car would expedite things.

However.

The three boys could be hiding close by. It could be a set-up. Except, Viktor didn't feel that they were close. In fact, Viktor had the feeling that they wouldn't know if he took the car. This left him with the problem of someone spotting him in the car should the boys have met with foul play.

Foul play? Viktor was suddenly certain that the young men were –

He reached through the window, thinking to grab the keys, but something else caught his eye, and he drew his hand back. He opened the car door and climbed inside, so he could reach into the passenger seat.

From the center of the seat, he plucked a small, silver dragonfly with multi-colored jade wings. It was attached to a sturdy piece of rolled black silk, like a –

"Hair tie," he whispered. He studied the small, pretty thing a moment longer before slipping it into a jean pocket. He shut the car door, and then started the engine.

He was feeling much more at ease when he backed the Renault out of the hiding place, and then took off down the road.

**

"So," Mitch said, when Damona opened the door and let Viktor in. "Get lucky or something?"

Viktor made no reply as he sat on the end of Damona's bed and picked up her copy of *Skid Marks*.

"Just out for a walk, then?" Mitch asked. Viktor hadn't taken the shitty car they'd gotten in France.

"Yes," the Rom replied. Mitch and Damona hadn't seen the sedan, and they wouldn't, because Viktor had dumped it outside the village and walked the rest of the way to the hotel.

"It was a nice night?" Damona asked, taking a spot beside him on the bed.

"Mmm." Viktor offered a short nod. There was no need to go into details, such as they were.

Mitch watched as his drummer placed a hand on Viktor's thigh, and let one of her fingers circle just above his knee before exploring closer to the inside of his thigh, at which the Rom's head turned and his piercing gaze met her doe-eyed stare.

Mitch had a sudden third wheel moment. "What say I scare up some breakfast?"

"Sure," said Viktor without looking away from Damona, and the blond suddenly felt dirty for watching them.

Maybe Viktor would at last cross the finish line. *I'll take my sweet time getting breakfast.*

"'Kay." Mitch didn't bother to ask what they wanted. They were predictable in that both of them considered coffee an absolute necessity and anything else was extra. Viktor in particular drank a whole lot of coffee, and Mitch had an idea why. "Be back in a bit," he said, and made a swift exit.

Mitch hoped they'd fuck and get it over with. He didn't know how much more tension he could take. *I don't know how the hell Vik stands it. I can't even handle watching. Well, maybe if they'd actually do something...*

He wandered on down the corridor, feeling (in his own mind, anyway) very un-French for leaving.

The couple in the hotel room were still gazing into each other's eyes. They hadn't realized that Mitch had left. They wouldn't have known if he were there, either. Damona's finger was still wandering and Viktor's breath had quickened the slightest bit. The comic book had been discarded on the floor with an automatic gesture and that free hand reached for Damona's face.

Her flesh crawled beneath his touch. He grazed her full lower lip with the pad of his thumb. She parted her lips in response; lips that so badly wished to feel the press of his. Lips that had yearned for months – years. Two long years.

She drew in a breath and held it when his lips moved closer. When Viktor dipped his head and slid his fingers down the side of her neck, her breath released in a soft moan. He was close. So close that she could taste the clove he must have smoked on the way back to the hotel. It was there, sickly sweet and spicy on his exhale, and she longed to grab fistfuls of his hair and yank him down on top of her.

But she couldn't. She wouldn't, because more than this, she burned for him to master her, and then there was the fear. Not fear of Viktor, but the fear of being rebuked and how much it would hurt. He had to choose. She'd always sensed this. Before he ever, in his cryptic way, spoke of being dangerous, she'd known this.

Viktor had to make the final move. As she felt his lips burn a trail into her skin from cheek to base of neck, she wondered if he was ready at last, if he was ready to trust that all would be well.

These thoughts became fevered, chanted pleas that perhaps he could sense. She felt a delicate touch to her left breast. A more insistent moan left her when that touch became more urgent.

Possessive.

Her entire body yielded even while her arms went around his neck as if of their own accord to hold him tight, lest he change his mind.

As for Viktor, he was awash in her scent. A musky scent always peppered with a hint of dark earth and cardamom. It drove him mad. Her skin was like milk, but she scented of headier things, and it drove him mad, the mystery and allure of it.

He could feel her giving over, and this too, drove him mad. He could sense, as he explored the taste of her mouth now in earnest, her need, her desire for him to claim her. Just take her then and there, to hell with the foreplay.

It was with a pained groan that he pulled away. It was with supreme effort that he stood and moved back from the temptation of her there on the bed, his focus on her upturned face, on her half-lidded eyes, which now flew open, and in a flash speared him with the sharpness of their disappointment, before the tranquil stare she had long ago perfected, took its place.

"I'm sorry," he said, his voice yet thick with lust. It wasn't the first time he'd nearly given in, and it wasn't the first time he'd apologized. She had told him each time that it was okay. *Don't be sorry.*

But this time she said, "What's that in your hand?"

He looked at his left hand. As soon as he did, the sensation of the weight of an object made itself known. He'd forgotten. Wasn't certain when he'd palmed it to begin with. But when he uncurled his long fingers, there it was, the dragonfly hair tie.

"Something I found," he said, staring at the trinket.

"Where?" Damona sounded rather normal. She'd gotten good at swift recoveries from childhood, on. Though with Viktor it was becoming more and more difficult to bounce back.

Her question brought his attention back to her. It wasn't an odd question, just odd having two in a row from her.

"I forget," he lied, not wanting to explain the entirety of his evening, some of which he still didn't remember.

"Another mystery," she commented. Neutral in tone, though the comment carried its own weight.

Viktor searched and searched her golden-brown eyes. He questioned, not for the first time, why it was that he didn't tell her more about himself, because with Damona, it was different. He felt a genuine trust between them, had since day one. He felt that she was a woman he could trust with his feelings, his truth.

But as usual, he came up with the one reply that always ended the conversation in his head.

He couldn't truly be with her, and so he couldn't truly share himself. Like what he'd just done on the bed, it wasn't right. It would be cruel. Cruel to share himself completely and then…

Besides. He couldn't do it to himself, either. The idea hurt. He knew that their time might be coming to a close. That he probably should move on and let Mitch and Damona move on in their own lives without him.

Yet…he hadn't been able to pry himself away from these two particular people, though he'd been trying to for over a year. More than a year.

"Now I'm sorry," Damona said, breaking the death grip of silence.

Viktor shook his head. "Don't be." He slipped the dragonfly into his pocket and started for the door. "I'll be in my room. Mitch can bring breakfast to me if he wants. If not, I don't care."

"Just the coffee," she whispered. "You need the coffee."

Viktor's hand paused in mid-reach for the doorknob. He looked back at her. "Yes. The coffee. Always the coffee."

"It's okay if I bring it?" Damona didn't beg. But her gaze did, and something inside of Viktor felt like it literally snapped.

"Yes." He grasped the knob. "Damona..." his gaze faltered and he turned the door knob. "Never mind."

After he'd exited, leaving her alone and in no need of keeping a brave face, Damona quietly addressed the spot he'd just vacated.

"I love you, too."

Maybe one day he'd say it, so she could say it to his face.

8

Viktor looked into the darkness of the cavernous room. A room that didn't carry the rancid yellow stench of piss and nicotine.

Smoking of any kind was forbidden in this place. Drugs, on the other hand, were welcome. Viktor mused that they were encouraged. Anyone who got carried away was, well... carried away.

Viktor didn't know as much about the club as he would've liked, but he remembered a few things from his other visits. There had been only two, but they had been interesting affairs, which still left an impression over three years later.

The Asian had brought him to this place called *The Fall Out*. Kar had discovered that Viktor made music and had introduced him to three others who learned songs faster than most and played several instruments. They were also quite good. No, they were great. Fantastic. And like Kar, Viktor hadn't seen them since he woke up in California.

He seemed to recall that his neck hairs had stood at attention around those temporary band-mates. They all shared that same glint in their eyes. Even the twins. There had been twins with such a unique look that no one could possibly forget them.

Viktor sipped at his drink while he watched Damona and Mitch dance. Or some approximation thereof. It looked more like riding a wave. One that turned half circles, swallowed them up, and then spit them out, over and over again. So many bodies on the sunken oval floor, it was only when they were vomited out that Viktor could see them. Such was the lighting, that he couldn't even track Damona's hair. They weren't so much dancing together as with one amorphous blob.

They'd been received rather well onstage. But this club was open until dawn, and not even *Satan's Whore* could keep a crowd interested for hours. Not this crowd, anyway.

Viktor drained the last of the liquid from his glass and slid off the metal-topped barstool, his attention back on the dance floor, and his intention: to dance with Damona for as long as he could stand, then find a place to relieve his *tension*. He studied the crowd, and just managed to locate the missing couple, or so he thought. Strobes had begun to flash, and Viktor was now uncertain.

"Oh man, I'm sweating to death," Mitch yelled. With the pulsing industrial wave of music, Damona still didn't understand him. Not that it mattered. She could likely guess, he thought.

Unsure, Mitch carried on nonetheless, figuring that his bodily functions were of little interest to his dance partner. Or partners. He could hardly tell where one arm started and another ended.

"I'm gonna get a drink!" Mitch leaned in close. Well, closer than he already was. "Want one?"

Coppery hair swung side to side as she shook her head. Hair that begged for attention. Mitch thought she understood him well enough. Or maybe she was just dancing; it was difficult for her band-mate to tell. He shrugged and began the task of squishing through the bodies, not bothering with *pardon me, excuse me, sorry*. They wouldn't hear him any better than Damona had. He merely nodded where appropriate.

"Fuck, at this rate it'll take me an hour." The blond laughed at himself and continued to press – occasionally against a well-formed body, which he didn't mind at all. Someone familiar then came into view.

"Hey Vik!" The guitarist shook his head at himself, wondering why he'd even bothered. Habit, he supposed. Impulse. Still, it looked to Mitch as if the gypsy was looking back in his direction, so he yelled once more.

"Viktor!"

The bass player did, in fact, notice his guitarist, if not hear him. He sluiced through the edge of the crowd, closing in on the oval's perimeter. He came to an abrupt halt. Something, just there, in the corner of his eye, had captured his attention; but when he turned his head in its direction, he couldn't pick anything out in the sea of flesh, leather, lace, and other sweat-shined fabrics.

Viktor thought about this for a moment, allowing people to press in on him as they would. No resistance, no reprimands.

Mitch kept his eyes on Viktor, certain that the other man had seen him, and so puzzled as to why he'd stopped.

"Viktor!" he tried again, pressing forward. "Hey, Vik!"

Viktor shook himself and refocused on Mitch. Just as he began to move, take a step down closer to the actual dance floor, Viktor saw it again. There and gone. Mitch jumped up and down, waving his arms.

"Hang on, I'm coming," he said.

But Viktor took a sudden step to the left, and for a moment, Mitch lost sight of him. When his gaze landed on Viktor once more, the bass player was much farther away, and appeared to be heading toward the stairway, which led up to the insanely thick metal door that opened on a crappy little room with a crappy corrugated door. The exit/entrance.

What the fuck?

Drink forgotten, the blond decided to follow the brunet. Felt compelled to follow him, though he couldn't precisely explain why, and next he knew, he was standing outside, his salt-soaked shirt chill against his flesh in the night air.

Viktor himself had lost all awareness of anything other than what he was chasing. Thought he was chasing. He wasn't certain. He had chased a feeling more than a vision. Had felt drawn along, and was just now realizing that the air was cooler and the surroundings, quieter.

Mitch watched in fascination as Viktor drifted farther away from the building towards the excuse for a road. He opened his mouth to call his name when the taller man stepped *into* the road. Stepped into it and came to a stop, right in the middle of it. But the blond quickly snapped his mouth shut. It felt as though he might break a spell if he said anything. He couldn't do that. He needed to see what else the Rom was going to do.

Mitch himself was under spell, for he whispered his friend's name without thought, without awareness, but neither did Viktor notice. He continued to stand in the middle of that road, wondering where the man had gone. If there ever had been a man, that is, and not just a shadow in his peripheral. Not just a hope manifesting as a delusion.

Someone did approach, someone Mitch saw first and Viktor sensed, but this someone was no man. It was a tall, cool woman with long pale hair and eyes blue and bright as a Popsicle. If she'd seen Mitch, she ignored him, and so, apparently, did Viktor when he turned and let his gaze roam over the red satin clad beauty.

"Good evening," she said, her voice as tantalizing as a tongue on an earlobe. "Are you looking for something? Perhaps, even, someone?"

Viktor's study of her extended past the satin that stopped mid-thigh, before he lifted his eyes to meet her gaze. "Someone? You mean someone like you?"

Her smile broke wide, ruby lips glistening. "Yes. Someone *exactly* like me." She slinked closer. "I was looking for you, after all."

Only a few feet away, the other blond wanted to protest. He'd had the sudden, irresistible urge to flee, just before the woman had spoken, but her seductive tones had fixed him to the spot. Still, he had some of his wits – perhaps because she wasn't speaking directly to *him*.

Mitch wanted to walk up to Viktor and grab his arm, tell him that Damona was looking for him. He couldn't seem to. He wanted to call out his name, ask him to come inside for a drink. He couldn't seem to.

Maybe she'd put a spell on him, after all.

Mitch stood in place, watched as Viktor smiled a dark smile and took the woman's hand. Stood, helpless, as the two began to walk away.

He managed to find his voice after they'd taken a few steps.

"Vik! Aren't you coming back inside?"

The headshake, the look and the smile he received in response, were unsettling as hell – and they didn't come from Viktor, who gave him only a glance.

"Damona will be so disappointed," Mitch said. To himself. The other two had drifted quite swiftly away, and there was no point in yelling, because Mitch knew that look. Mitch knew that Viktor wasn't coming back for several hours, at least.

If he could just shake the creepy feeling and figure out where it came from, he'd feel a lot better. Unable to do so, he took his time returning to the club. He didn't want Damona to notice his concern, especially as he had no explanation for it that made sense. As for Vik taking off with some other woman, well.

Damona was used to it, Mitch knew. Whether she was okay with it, was another story. He didn't think so. Best to keep it to himself as long as he could get away with.

9

Sweat. Musk. Blood.
Blood. Musk. Sweat.
Cool flesh.
Hot flesh.
Arms and legs entwined, no beginning, no end.
Hissing, growling, grunting.
Pleasure.

Finally a deep cry. Another, as if having taken so long to bring the first, once the dam opened there was a flood. Another, another.
A change in tone, throat is tightening, tightening.

Pain.
Pain, pain, more pain, and a deep dark well burst up like a geyser.
Deep, dark, very cold water, like the deepest ocean, where unseen things slither in a place that truly has no light.

Flash of steel, honed to sharpness near as precise as a scalpel. Just a flash, before it is hilt deep between the breasts of all too white flesh above.
Eyes. Watching, with fascination, the crystalline red jewels that begin to dance along that flesh.

Feeling, with some perverted sense of enjoyment, the movement that brings the blade upward without leaving this solid flesh, dissecting things internally until...the heart.

Cold eyes watch the fire above in the other eyes dim, dim, dim. And then go out as if snuffed.

Numbness. Blood covered limbs register, but numb. Covered in blood and the now lifeless body.

Lifeless body.
Lifeless.
It's felt. Hardness inside her. Still hard inside the –

DEAD BODY.

She's nearly dumped on the floor when understanding hits.

Off the bed, eyes wide, speechless, confused, mortified, a different cry scalds the chest.

Don't look, don't look, don't look!

"Sylvan!"

Viktor woke with her name dying on his lips, the name of a woman he'd known for all of one night. She was the star of a nightmare he recalled all too well in both waking and sleeping life. He remembered the blood; so much blood, and her lifeless body, legs limp on either side of him, erection yet deep in her flesh, just as his long blade was yet in her flesh.

Her still warm flesh.

What he didn't remember was killing her. He didn't know what had snapped, why he'd done it, or how, except that he'd clearly stabbed her.

More than stabbed her, judging from the mess of her torso.

There had been pleasure, there had been pain, and there had been blackness. Then a dead body that yet encased his cock.

Mortified as he was, she'd hit the floor with a thump when he'd scrambled to get out of her, out from beneath her, and flown from the bed. Flown from the room. A desire he had now.

He wanted to get out of the body, off the bed, away from –

A cry tripped over a second cry vying to escape Viktor's throat.

It wasn't a nightmare.

Not just a nightmare then, not a nightmare, now.

He'd done it again. Again.

Viktor stared down in abject horror at the face of the tall, cool woman he'd gone home with. Her Popsicle blue eyes, frozen wide, stared back at him, dim and uncomprehending. There was no need to check her pulse, no need to say her name – whatever it was – because there was no life, not a spark, in her gaze. Not a twitch in her muscles.

There was also the undeniable fact that his hand yet rested on the hilt of his serrated long knife, the only visible part of the weapon. When he had plunged it into her chest, he did not know.

He yanked his hand back with a mouthed cry, the metal catching on her breastplate as he did so, and it made a sound that only a knife on bone could make. Her viscera sucked at the blade on the way out, a sound familiar, perhaps, to butchers, chefs and haggard women the world over.

Bile rose in his throat when the gaping maw of her chest demanded his attention. He swallowed in convulsions as he looked into the muddy red, rust and pink colored hole where her heart lived.

Or had.

Viktor's stomach turned inside out. He couldn't stop its contents from gushing out to fill the spot her heart had vacated. The spot he must have cut it from, torn it away, done – done God knows what, with it. In the miasma of the moment, he had the nauseating thought that maybe he'd eaten it, and now was replacing it.

He puked repeatedly, until nothing but acidic, greenish liquid dribbled out, which didn't take long, as he'd not eaten much to begin with, though to Viktor it seemed an eternity. The following dry heaves nearly split him in two.

Fitting, perhaps.

He managed at last to roll off the body. He hit the floor with a bone-rattling smack, his knife yet caught in his claw-like grip. It was as if his fingers had their own rigor mortis setting in.

"Jesus what have you done, you sick fuck?" Viktor tried to loosen his grip on the knife. When his fingers wouldn't obey, he slammed the side of his hand against the floor. "Sick fuck!" Slam. "Sick!" Slam. "Fuck!" Metal clanged, skittered across the hard floor.

Tears sprang and leaked from the corners of his eyes. Something that rarely ever happened to Viktor. He'd learned long ago that crying didn't get him anywhere. He'd grown skin as thick as an elephant's. He'd accepted his fate, whatever it was.

But Sylvan was five years ago. He would always be sorry for it, but he'd gotten past it, except for the nightmares, and after Sylvan, he'd been celibate. Except for that one time. He'd sworn that he wouldn't have sex, let alone fall asleep. And he hadn't. Fallen asleep. He didn't think that he had. The more he tried to clear his mind, the cloudier things became.

One thing was clear. He'd broken his promise.

Viktor let go and wept in earnest. Something he hadn't let himself do since he was a child. He was so tired, so confused, so damned sorry. His gaze wandered to the bed. To the spill of hair that trailed across what was left of a breast. She was slowly becoming a redhead, the blond strands stained with her blood, still soaking up her blood.

In the midst of his grief, arousal struck, swift and vicious as a cornered viper.

Viktor wanted to grab the offensive erection and rip it from his body. Instead, his fists flew to his temples and landed with a thud. "Why do I even go on? Sick, sick, sadistic pig."

"She was going to kill you."

Viktor's sobbing ceased. His breathing became shallow. His eyes darted towards the source of the voice.

"As you yet live," continued the voice, "you have proven yourself the fittest. A right and natural way of things."

Viktor stared at the shadow. His eyes couldn't discern the features belonging to the owner of the smooth, deep voice. But he was certain that he recognized it.

"This wasn't the Death I was seeking, either?" Viktor asked.

"No."

The form moved into the light, revealing a man nearly as tall as Viktor himself. A man with jet hair spilling over his shoulders, hanging about his waist. His eyes, two onyx marbles, fixed their gaze upon the knife that had slid close to his feet mere moments before.

"This time, you didn't arrive here of your own volition," said the Asian.

When Viktor looked up into the face of the man he most often referred to as Savior, everything else fell away. Thoughts that perhaps he didn't deserve to live. That he himself was a demon. That his mother's prophecy was too long in coming. It all fell away, because he couldn't believe he'd actually found – been found – by the man called Kar.

Yet it felt so normal. Natural. Right.

"I didn't arrive in the catacombs under my own power, either," Viktor managed to say.

Kar's eyes lifted. He offered the other man a faint smile. "You know what I mean."

Viktor glanced at the body on the bed. A body that had already been cold, he realized, when he'd come to his senses and understood what he'd done.

A body that perhaps was always cold, he thought, though he wasn't certain why it came to mind.

"She charmed you into coming home with her," the Asian said, his tone cool and clinical.

"Don't they always?" Viktor replied.

"She had a special type of charm."

Viktor's gaze swung back to his mysterious companion.

"Do not worry over it." Kar gestured towards the bed. "No one needs to know of this."

"It appears I ripped out her heart, and you're telling me not to worry?" Viktor let out a sick sounding laugh.

The regal Asian studied the man yet sitting on the floor, whose body was painted with the woman's drying blood, strands of her hair caught beneath his fingernails. Dark eyes took it all in, every minute detail. So much so that the one they studied began to feel nude in a very different way.

"You didn't worry overmuch about those slain in the catacombs," Kar said at last.

"They weren't pretty women out for a sport fuck."

Kar's mouth hinted at a wry smile. "Neither was she. Out for a sport fuck, as you so eloquently put it."

Viktor felt an absurd urge to apologize for his language. Absurd considering the circumstance. Also absurd, he thought, was the fact he was less and less uncomfortable being in the presence of a woman he'd vivisected while screwing.

He was sick; he knew it. He must be.

"How long have you been here?" he asked. Something he needed to know, regardless of his other urges. There were many things he needed to know. Perhaps his Savior would enlighten him on a few points.

"Long enough."

Viktor came to his feet and looked the other man in the eye. "For what? To enjoy a show? Did you plan it? You seem to know her."

The semi-stranger arched a brow at Viktor.

"Maybe you did it," Viktor said.

The reply was calm. Cool. "You know that I didn't. You know that it was you."

Viktor had the urge to grab the other man's shoulders and shake him; shake him until his innards fell out. He did no such thing. "Why didn't you stop me? You were here, weren't you? Why didn't you stop me?"

Kar's gaze pierced Viktor's own, the Asian's giving off a glint in the candlelit room. "She was capable of defending herself."

"Clearly not!"

"At first, I was concerned for *you*. Clearly, there was no need for concern on my part."

Viktor could only stare into those hypnotic eyes.

Kar said, "Normally, she would be quite safe with someone such as you. So to speak."

"You confuse me," Viktor whispered. "I've murdered someone you know, yet you're acting as if I've done nothing wrong. You seem even to be…" Viktor shook his head.

"Impressed? Yes. I am duly impressed."

"You're sicker than I."

Kar offered the first full smile of the exchange. "Not at all. There is something quite interesting going on with you, to be certain. But you acted in self-defense. Does this soothe you?"

Viktor had no idea what was soothing him, but when he thought about it, he understood that he was rather calm and collected for someone who had just –

"I am calm. This proves it. I'm psychotic." Viktor desperately wanted Kar to say that he wasn't, even if it was a lie. "I'm a psychopath. It looks like I enjoyed defending myself."

"I do not think so," the Asian replied. "You wept. It was genuine."

"Self-defense, you said. What was she doing, fucking me to death?" Viktor tried to laugh at his own twisted joke.

Kar's expression smoothed. "Your instincts are sharp. As were her teeth."

Viktor stood there, blinking at the other man.

"Viktor. You know what she is." The dark gaze moved towards the bed, and back. "Was."

Viktor studied Kar's expression. His eyes. His skin.

"And you were looking for me," said Kar. "Here I stand. I always knew that you would return one day. I must say you've made some interesting choices in the last three years."

Viktor's breath came in a quiet gasp of understanding. "The dragonfly. It's yours."

Kar offered a regal nod of his head.

"You haven't been watching just since I arrived. You've always been watching," Viktor said.

The nod came once more.

"What are you?" Viktor moved closer to the other man. Close enough to see the pores in that pale flesh. Except there weren't any. "Some kind of personal guardian?"

"I note you did not say angel. Demon would be the word on your tongue, normally." Kar inclined his head. "I have seen you in the last three years, yes. Because I find your situation interesting."

"My situation. Can you tell me what my situation is?"

Cool fingers came to Viktor's shoulder. "I might have a theory. So might some friends of mine."

Viktor's knees weakened with the idea that his Savior truly might have some answers for him after all.

10

Mitch paced another tight circle while Damona blew out a lazy swirl of smoke. She didn't smoke often, but when she did, it wasn't cloves. Lucky's, when she could find them. Unfiltered. Mitch thought that was rather hardcore for a chick, or so he'd told her, once. But Mitch mostly smoked cloves, which Damona thought was 'pussy,' since he was only imitating Viktor.

She watched him finish another circle and rolled her eyes.

"Are you going to do this until the sun rises?" she asked. "It became old the first two trips around."

Mitch stopped, walked directly to her, and looked her hard in the eyes. "Aren't you worried? Just a little?"

The redhead shrugged and had another drag off her cigarette.

"Seriously," Mitch said. "Do you even care?"

Her cool gaze turned into a glare, and she blew a puff of smoke straight into his face. Coughing, Mitch fanned the smoke away.

"Okay, okay, sorry. Stupid question," he said.

"Very stupid," she agreed.

He studied her. "At least I got a rise out of you. You're too damned – I don't know. Too damned tranquil all the time. It's freaky, you know that?"

Damona's reaction was delayed. Mitch was startled when she threw her cigarette down, hard, and smashed it repeatedly underfoot.

"What am I to do?" she yelled, the sound pushing Mitch back a step. He'd never heard her yell. Not offstage, anyway.

"Tell me," she continued, clearly agitated. "What do I do? I can't leash him, I can't change him and I can't follow where he doesn't let me go!" She crossed her arms over her chest as if she were cold. "I can't see the path. He will not show me."

Mitch's shoulders sagged when Damona's eyes dropped and she studied the road kill of a cigarette butt by her foot. He hadn't meant to upset her. He hadn't thought it possible to upset her. He chastised himself for that. She had feelings, no shit she did. *Idiot. She just never lets me see how much she…*

"Damona, I'm sorry. Really. I didn't mean to…I'm sorry." He reached for her, but she remained frozen. "Damona…"

"Probably he is fucking her right now," she said, without looking up. "Probably they're laughing and drinking and he's telling her things." Her arms dropped to her sides. To Mitch she looked smaller, defeated. "But he owes me nothing, Mitch." She looked up into his eyes. "He owes me nothing. So I say nothing."

"But…" Mitch stepped closer to her. "Why don't you, Damona? Why don't you say something?"

She turned away. "You've met Viktor. You must ask me this?"

"Yeah, I must." He tossed his hands out from his sides. "You're *way* into him and he's way into you, so what the hell? Why the- the torture, huh?"

He barely heard her next, whispered words. "I thought you were sorry. But you say these things."

Mitch looked down at his shoes. "He still won't let you in. I know." The guitar-player considered just sitting down on the gravel, right there by the club. "After all this time I don't know him very well, either."

Damona directed a liquid gaze over her shoulder in her band-mate's direction. "You know pushing won't work. He'd only make more distance. So I don't push. Even if I want, I don't. It is torture, true. What would you have me do?"

Mitch shook his head, opting to plop down on his ass, after all. He lifted his gaze to his companion when she turned to face him.

"I'm sorry I stated the obvious and made you feel bad. I'm – I have a bad feeling about…" Mitch didn't want to state more obvious, hurtful things. "Well. I have bad feeling."

"So do I."

Her friend's eyes widened when she said it. She knew why. It wasn't often, if at all, that she said such things.

"He has stayed away many nights, before," she said. "But it feels different. Still two? Yes maybe two hours until dawn but it's different."

Mitch could do nothing but continue to stare at her for a few moments. So long did he stare, that she opted to plop down on the gravel beside him. He wasn't so far gone that he didn't notice the incredible view it afforded him of her thighs.

Latex hugged too well to ride up any higher, though. Viktor would've appreciated the view regardless, he knew.

Viktor. He didn't know what to say. Maybe it was best to sit with Damona in companionable silence. Maybe that's all she wanted or needed just now. She was often very good with silence. He was afraid he'd stick his foot in his mouth again, anyway. What was there to say, other than some more obvious bullshit?

She was right. Viktor was probably off fucking the tall blonde. Marathon sex, stopping every now and then for a sip of coffee.

Viktor drank a metric butt ton of coffee. When he wasn't drinking Chivas, that is.

"Tall and blonde," Damona said. "Maybe he don't like redheads."

"You know that's not true."

"Thank you for helping me out with that." Her tone was thick with sarcasm.

Mitch sighed. "Pretending there're other reasons isn't going to work, is it?" He shook his head. "I can't do it. If I was any good at it, I'd try helping you lie to yourself."

Damona rifled through her purse and found the pack of Lucky's and her lighter. Soon, she inhaled deeply of the cancer stick. She tossed the pack and lighter back into her purse, with little care. The lighter missed, skittering along the gravel.

She paid it no mind. Mitch noticed, but left it.

"What do you think his secret, is?" Damona asked. This surprised Mitch. Damona never pried. Not that this was prying, by most standards. For her to ask any such question – she'd probably call it prying. It was odd.

"I don't know," Mitch said. Except he wondered if that were true. He wondered if he should voice the opinion that came to him. Had she ever thought about it? She hadn't been there that Nevada night. She hadn't seen what he'd seen.

"It must be deep and dark," she said, through a haze of smoke.

"I wonder sometimes…"

Her gaze swung to him. He could feel it burning into his face. Well, he'd started it. He had the feeling that this time, she wouldn't let him redirect, let him get away with dropping it. No. She'd asked.

"I wonder sometimes," he said, "if he's wanted. If he's a fugitive."

Damona waved a hand. "That's too simple."

Mitch's brows shot up. "You think? What's simple about that?"

She shook her head as she sucked on the cigarette, leaving a cherry red ring around the end. More smoke laced through her words. "He's not afraid of police. We've run into them before. He wouldn't return to bars more than once. Not smart." She indulged in another drag. "Viktor is a very smart man."

Mitch couldn't disagree with that. Viktor was street smart as well as learned, and seemed to have good intuitions.

"Maybe they've never connected it to him," Mitch said, as an afterthought.

"What...?"

Mitch looked over to see Damona's hard, hard stare. One that made him shrink, almost literally. "Um..." It wasn't right, even if it was Damona. He'd never told anyone. Why did he say what he said aloud? A slip? A slip so he'd have to tell her?

On she stared. She wasn't letting this one slide.

"I saw him kill someone, once." When she didn't react, he said a few more words. "It was ugly."

That was an understatement.

Damona was still for so long, that Mitch wondered if she'd even heard him. If she'd understood. Or perhaps she was in shock. He regretted telling her, now. He couldn't discern what she might be thinking. Would she dump the band, now? Would she confront Viktor?

Maybe it would be a good thing, or maybe not. Viktor may never forgive him. Though his bass player didn't seem to remember the event...

Still, he'd know that Mitch said something bad, something secret, about him.

Damona's cigarette was close to singeing her fingertips. She flinched and tossed it away, lowering her gaze as she did so. Mitch felt the heat of it leave, and it was a relief. But he still wanted to know what she was thinking.

Had he fucked up royally?

"Maybe I killed someone too," she said at last. "Maybe so did you. He had a reason."

Mitch looked at her with widened eyes as she rose. Was she in denial? Or did she mean what she'd said. Had she killed someone? He sure as hell hadn't. Yes, he'd lied, stolen and cheated. He'd done some drugs. He'd even been in some brawls. But he hadn't killed anyone.

And what Viktor had done to the man who reached for his necklace…

Mitch shuddered, but Damona didn't see this. So she didn't ask. She'd turned her back to him, seemingly lost in thought. Mitch decided that she'd clammed up on the subject for the night, so he got up. Brushed the dust off the ass of his jeans, and wondered what to do, next.

The hotel? They'd checked. They could check again. After a glance at Damona, it seemed clear she was intent on staying put. Mitch wondered why he'd bothered to stand up if they were going to wait outside *The Fall Out* the rest of the night. Or morning. It was so far into the a.m. he guessed dawn would break, and soon.

Damona rubbed her bare arms.

"Cold?" Mitch asked. "You can have my jacket."

She shook her head. Mitch shrugged. He'd asked her three times before, with the same result. It depressed him. He knew she pined away for Viktor in some sense, or guessed that she did, but he'd never seen her so down. It had never been so obvious.

She'd never been so…vulnerable.

"Forget what I said," Mitch whispered. "About Vik."

She snorted.

Yeah, I know, Mitch thought. *How do you forget someone telling you the man you love is a killer?*

"He is afraid he will hurt me," Damona said. "Now I know it's for real. That he didn't just mean my heart." She turned her gaze to her companion. "I've known there is something dark. I always sensed. Something…there is something. What you said, I'm not surprised."

Just when Mitch was certain she'd clammed up. He could only look at her, afraid that if he said a word, she'd close up shop, again.

"I know you wonder," she continued. "Why he never sleeps in the same room. Why he drinks so much coffee. Why he always drives."

"I know he has nightmares," Mitch said. "He told me that much, once. So I figure he wants to stay awake. Guess they must be bad."

She nodded. "Very. It's not so much what he says. It's what he doesn't say about them. If you can see between the words, the…the lines, you can guess many things."

Mitch knew just what she meant.

"You saw him kill someone but you don't tell. You stay with him," she said.

Mitch wasn't sure how to explain it. He contemplated his next words.

"Maybe…maybe some of the same reasons you'll end up staying, regardless of what I just told you," he said.

Damona almost smiled. It seemed that they understood each other, at least on this score.

"Different type of horror film," he said. "One where the victims are willing?"

She laughed. He could always count on her to go with the dark humor, which was why he'd said it. It had gotten too heavy for Mitch.

Shame she had one more question.

"Was it very bad?" she asked, and Mitch knew what she meant. "Did he go crazy on the person?"

"He…it didn't seem like him. And that sounds like I'm defending him. But, what you know of him, it makes some sense, yeah? Though he knows he's dangerous. I mean, he *says* he is. So he must have some idea…"

His drummer's brows knit.

"Yeah, that was babble. What I mean is," Mitch moved closer to her, "I don't think he knew what he was doing. It was so surreal. I swear that's not some made up shit, either, to comfort myself. It's not me having some moment of disbelief. Because I've thought hard about it. It really, really didn't seem like he knew what he was doing."

Damona turned and closed in on Mitch. "You don't think he knows even now?"

Mitch spread his hands. "I know it sounds weird. It sounds like he's crazy."

"He's made comments like, like – he might lose control in some way with me. Not often, but when he drops his guard," she said. "See? It's not his fault."

Mitch shook and shook his head. "Man. You realize there's something wrong with us, too, right? We're looking for excuses. We know he's not right in the head, but here we are, the willing disciples."

"But it means he's sick, needs help, hmm?" Damona's gaze dropped. She studied the toes of her boots. She shrugged. "But I never said I was right, like you put it, either."

"No, but you're not a killer. I'm pretty sure you're not, anyway."

She flicked her gaze in his direction. "Neither are you." She looked down, with another shrug of shoulders. "But I don't have anyone else." She peeked up at him. "Besides, there's something very good in Viktor. There is much to the story. Maybe you tell me all of what happened. Because you're still with him longer than me."

Mitch nodded, and studied the old warehouse. He would tell her the story, all of it. Now that he'd told the secret, he couldn't hide the details forever. She hadn't reacted that badly to his initial reveal. Not like any normal person, might. But neither had he. Because a normal person would have run off at the very least, and called the cops, at most, three years ago.

He was about to do the once upon a time thing, figuring she could handle the details (though maybe then she'd have a normal reaction to those, but she deserved the truth), when she made a strange, small sound. He turned his head in her direction and saw that she was staring with wide eyes just past him.

His own eyes widened after he turned to see what she was looking at. Viktor, striding pretty as you please, in their direction.

"You're still here." Viktor walked up to, and then past them. "Rental still over there?"

Damona and Mitch exchanged a look. Mitch followed Viktor. Damona started after them, remembered her purse, and trotted up behind them after retrieving it. Just in time to hear Viktor say:

"No big thing. I'm tired. I want to get to the hotel."

Mitch glanced at Damona. Sure, Viktor had shown up like this before – nonchalant, as if nothing was amiss. For all they knew, there wasn't. Damona wasn't going to make a deal of it, and Mitch figured he couldn't press for details.

So Viktor had stayed out. Nothing new. It was just that his pals had been wallowing in dark places while he'd been off doing whatever it was he did. It didn't seem the same, but neither of them could explain why.

So there was no use confronting Viktor. It hadn't gotten Mitch anywhere the last time, when Viktor strolled up to the hotel after dawn. Sans car. Now *that*, had been a bit strange, but then again, it was Vik.

Viktor paused in his stroll to look at his band-mates. "What?"

Mitch glanced at Damona, a very telling gesture, but Damona was the less obvious of the two (always) and held Viktor's gaze.

She offered him a shrug. "I don't know. What?"

Mitch mimicked her shrug.

Viktor looked between them. He had a sense they'd been commiserating over something when he arrived. That perhaps he'd interrupted.

As Viktor didn't feel like explaining where he'd just come from, and with whom he'd been (not to mention the dead woman he came to inside), he let it go. Whatever they'd been talking about couldn't compare to his night in importance.

Not that they weren't important people.

"Well, then." Viktor resumed his path towards the car.

11

A face, burning hot. No sunshine. Heat, it comes from exertion. From anger. From pain.

Fire. And fire dots the hillside. Torches.

Bodies. Not yet, but the eye sees it littered with dead bodies in place of the living. A future vision.

A hoarse scream that comes from the very bowels of despair. It forms a word, recognizable only in the mind of the one that makes the sound.

The scream comes again. Again.

Hot wetness. Cheeks stinging hot, as if lit with one of the very torches that wave frantically about, a frantic dance of shadow and light.

Cloth.

Scrap.

Scrap of cloth, suddenly clutched in a hand that's lost its glove.

Inhale. Scent. Scent.

The little yellow flowers.

The fresh, clean spring of perfect flesh.

BLOOD!

Despair.
Despair.

ANGER.

The word, a name, a name, screamed loud and long.

Despair.
Becomes Fury.

Rage.

It cuts a swath through flesh, any flesh. Flesh and bone, on a razor's edge of metal.

Screaming. Begging.
All ignored, yet heard.

AWAY FROM HER!

Cries of Master, Master reduced to gurgling gibberish.

A Demon from hell moves over the landscape, shredding all in his path.
They try to flee, to no avail. Rage leaves none untouched. It destroys every living thing that is not the one Hope seeks.

Rage, such rage.
Such Despair.

What heart that still beat in the Demon's chest shatters for all time, for what once was the last thing that could keep it pieced together, has fled.

Was taken.
Taken.
Sweet glimmer of the last light...the one last, small light that could have grown-
Is gone.
Red. Vision bathed in red...red and black.

She stumbled back when he leaped from the bed, thunderous words in a language she didn't understand, hurled in her direction. She'd never been afraid of him, but there was a hard, wild look in his eyes. It made her scramble back, back, until she ran into the door.

He didn't come after her. Not at all. He ransacked the bed, tearing the covers off, the sheets, and flung them to the floor. As she took a trembling breath, it occurred to her that he looked to be searching for something.

It seemed a good guess, when he began pulling at the dresser drawers, and, not finding what he wanted, slammed them shut with such force they splintered.

That he found nothing seemed to anger him more. She nearly jumped out of her skin with the explosion of glass. It took her frantic mind more than a moment to reason that he'd launched a bedside lamp at the dresser. It prepared her for the second crash, but she was almost as startled by that sound, as the first.

Again a string of words. She couldn't make out a single thing. She didn't know what he was talking about, but one thing she did begin to understand, was that he didn't seem to be talking to her.

In fact, he didn't seem like himself at all. As fear and shock turned more and more to curiosity, she became certain that the man she was looking at, wasn't quite Viktor.

She was more right than she knew. But she lost her train of thought when he wailed in grief and sank to the floor.

**

Viktor found himself in a sitting position, knees hugged to his chest. A ball of tears, a weight on his chest, and a rage just tempered. *Just* tempered, he realized when he lifted his face, and saw the shambles of his hotel room. A vision he had expected to meet with, because the feeling was familiar. It had happened enough times that surprise no longer claimed him when he saw a tornado wrecked room.

He'd made quite the work of it. He'd need to pay for the damage. But whatever calculations he'd been about to make, flew from his mind, when his gaze landed on another living person, huddled by the door.

He sat up straight, and in a blur of movement, was on his feet. Red, red hair drew him to the spot.

"Damona, what…why are you…" He started to reach for her, and his fingertips stopped just shy of her face. "Are you okay? Oh no…are you all right?" A knot formed in his stomach.

She nodded, staring wide-eyed at him. He was too distraught and confused to note the sadness in those wide eyes. The concern.

"Are you sure?" His fingertips closed the remaining distance to find her cheek. When she didn't flinch, the knot in his stomach loosened.

"I wouldn't worry about me. You, on the other side…"

"You mean hand." It was automatic, his correction. He studied her. She seemed fine. Physically. Clearly, she could see the mess of the room. Now he needed to know…

"How did you get in here, Damona?"

"I'm sorry; just I worried, so I came in."

"It's okay." Though it was the first time she'd ever been that forward. She must have been terribly concerned. "But how did you get in here?" Previous night's events with the creatures must have worn him out enough to oversleep.

"There were two card keys. I took one when you didn't see."

Of course. He nodded. Of course. "How long…"

"Have I been here? Long enough, I think."

Seemed to be the stock answer to that question. By her expression, he'd have to agree that she'd been there long enough. "I'll understand if you want to leave." He began to rise.

She reached and grabbed his arm. "I mean to see." Her gaze moved about the room. "Long enough to see you do this."

"Yes. Like I said."

She shook her head. "I don't need to leave. I won't leave you this way."

Viktor squatted back down. "I'm fine."

"I don't think so."

He couldn't debate that, in truth. "I…don't know what to say."

She searched his eyes. "This is why you won't stay with me."

He opted to nod. It was true enough, just not all of the truth. It wasn't this specific nightmare that most concerned him. It was what he'd done just last night. That he was trying very hard not to think about, lest it show in his eyes.

Exercise in futility, though his Savior had talked him down quite a bit.

"You were so violent," she said. "And like you're looking for something."

He nodded again.

"You know?"

"Not precisely. But it makes sense, in a way."

She filed his response away, and continued with the thoughts that had rushed through her while watching him.

"But it doesn't seem like you. It didn't seem like you knew what you were doing. Out of control –"

"Sleep walking."

She searched his eyes once again. Harder. "Okay. Sleep walking."

She wasn't buying it. He could see this. But he had no other explanation, because nothing else made sense, other than him being insane.

"Damona –"

"I know."

His eyes narrowed. "You know what?"

"You're ill. Maybe? You should do that, what is it, they do sleep studies?"

His eyes narrowed a bit more, and for the first time since he'd known her, Damona looked nervous. Fidgety under his gaze. She only ever fidgeted under his gaze when...

He kissed her. Hard. Claimed her mouth and left his mark, lest anyone attempt to tread where he'd been. They'd find him there if they dared.

A sweet, surprised little moan left her, filling his mouth. He swallowed this down, and the next that came when he grabbed her face. When he memorized every taste bud and then did it over again, just in case there was a pop quiz, later.

He stood up, pulling her to her feet along with him. Wrapped her up tight, so tight, in his arms. He was nude, as he always was when he slept. The flimsy fabric of her tap pants did little to separate the obvious arousal between them. She could feel every inch of him, hot, like she was. Her leg slid up one of his, independent of her will, trying to find its way around his hip. A desperate attempt to invite more contact with his hardness. To open the way.

She let go with a sound of frustration, right after another sharp moan.

He was so tall. Her body practically slithered up his, or tried. She grasped his shoulders and lifted, pulled, tried to climb, without separating herself from his mouth. Or his hands, which were all over her, it seemed, his touch possessive, and frantic. As if to let go, meant losing her forever.

His hands came to her ass, cupping it. Her heart raced at mach 5. He was helping her. Returning the invitation. He'd sink into her and quench the fire that sparked when they met, and now was an inferno.

At last, at last, at last – this was the rhythm of her breath.

"Yes, oh yes, please…" Damona panted these words into his mouth, and groped for every patch of flesh within her reach.

It was abrupt, like a gunshot, when he broke the kiss and walked away. A sound of anguish, pain, followed him. Damona didn't know if she'd made the sound, or him. Or both of them. She stood, trembling, with so many feelings, in such dire need, that she didn't know what to do, say, or whether to move.

Whether or not she *could* move. It turned out that she could, if only to wilt to the floor when her knees gave out.

Viktor stood with his back to her, hugging himself. A fine shiver still ran through him. He wanted her, wanted her with such force it ached in the pit of his belly, and this ache ran all the way through his body.

Tasting her, touching her, let him know that she was real, and that she was there. It helped his waking mind. It eased the pain in his chest. Though not completely. She wasn't in the dreams, he didn't think. She wasn't what he'd lost.

He didn't think. If she were, why would part of him feel so empty after that kiss? But it anchored him to the moment, to the reality of this world, even though it created a different pain in his heart.

But he'd almost let go. Almost taken her down to the floor and ravished her. Desire was a volcano ready to erupt, but then he'd seen his knife buried in a desecrated breast, and a deep blush spreading over pale hair.

"Damona, I…I…" he turned to face her. His expression fell when he saw her on the floor. Fell along with his heart.

"I'm sorry." He wanted to go to her. He didn't know if he should, after what he'd done. The impulse he'd followed.

It seemed all she could do was make a sound of such supreme frustration that his eyes moistened. There was no making up for such a cruel tease, though he hadn't meant for it to be.

"Damona…maybe if I told you…I should tell you…"

She rose, at last, animating all at once. "No. You shouldn't." She reached for the door.

"But…"

"Don't speak," she said with a violent shake of her head.

His face went into his hands. "Fuck. I know I shouldn't have done that."

"You shouldn't have stopped!"

He lowered his hands. He could only stare.

"Viktor…"

He held a breath.

She blew him a kiss. "See you for coffee? Twenty minutes?"

He offered a nod, his expression, incredulous.

"Okay." She opened the door and slipped out into the hallway.

Viktor stood, staring at the door, for several moments. He rubbed his face until it turned pink. He couldn't understand how she did it. How she switched gears like that.

Then again, he had no idea what coffee in twenty minutes might be like. Full of tension, perhaps. He'd do her the courtesy of showing up, though. If Mitch was there, he might get closer to what they spoke of last night when he was…

His mind switched its own gears and backed up.

Something had passed between her and Mitch last night. He knew it. He'd seen it in her eyes before he'd given over to lust and assurance. He'd almost confessed it, after, to explain why...

That wouldn't explain why he'd stopped. But it could work. It could work, so he'd not have to explain the women.

How many murders did it take to convince someone you were dangerous? To convince someone that you were bad, bad news. To make them be the ones who walked away, so you wouldn't have to?

Viktor knew what Mitch had seen. It was the reason Viktor himself had some idea of what he'd done. He'd gone away, that's what Mitch had called it. He'd 'gone away' and performed a little vivisection, a disembowelment, on some poor slob he didn't remember meeting. Or speaking to, for that matter.

Mitch hadn't spoken of it again after those first two days. When he *had* gathered enough wits to explain to Viktor what he'd done, Mitch tried to make less of it. He'd not offered all the details, not at first.

Viktor had pressed him for those minutiae. Viktor sometimes thought that Mitch spilled it because he was afraid not to. Afraid of Viktor.

Yet he hadn't left him. Mitch hadn't left him, and so far, no one had come looking for Viktor.

But in Damona's eyes, he'd seen it. She knew. Mitch must've told her. He didn't know why, after two years, he would. Then again, it was a terrible burden, such a heavy secret. He understood needing to unload it. Who better, than Damona? Whom else could Mitch talk to about it?

But she hadn't run away, either.

Well. Not yet, anyway.

12

Kar observed as the young man sipped at his scotch, contemplating the request he'd just made. Of all the people that he knew, vampire or no, this human was more likely to have some grasp of Viktor's situation.

Kar had offered to help Viktor. He had not offered a cure. He had no idea if there *was* a cure, even if they did ascertain what the mystery ailment, was.

"You're telling me this guy is basically a killer," the human said.

"Indeed, it is quite basic. He has killed, and so he is a killer. It's quite fascinating, really."

"You don't think he's just plain psychotic?" the young lawyer asked, and then held up a hand. "I'm not suggesting you're a bad judge of character. But if you don't mind humoring my normal, knee-jerk questions…"

Kar offered him a shake of his head. "Not at all. I understand."

"Okay. So you really don't think he's just…mental?"

"I know that he's not," Kar replied. "He feels remorse. He knows the difference between right and wrong."

"That doesn't mean he's not crazy."

Kar agreed. "This is true. But there are things at work here that have no explanation in your usual sciences."

No, he did not think that Viktor was insane. He never had. That explanation was far too simple, as it would happen. The

Rom clung to that self-diagnosis, at times, for lack of any other explanation; one of the few times being insane might be a comfort. Kar understood this need. Having an explanation was often the starting point for many people. Identifying the problem, meant that perhaps one could deal with it, if not change it.

It sometimes meant they had an excuse for their behavior, as well.

"And you don't think he enjoys what he's done?"

Kar worded his response carefully. "I do not think that Viktor does. But it's as if a secret part of him does. A hidden part."

The mortal studied the vampire. "You realize how that sounds."

"Of course. I do."

The young man nodded. "All right. Sounds to me like you need to give me the rest of the details. I can't just declare him possessed without details." He tossed back the rest of his drink. "Or without meeting him. That would be best."

"Then you'll do this, Master Trey?"

Trey du Bois offered up a wide grin, along with the slight shake of his head. "How many times do I have to say, *just Trey*. Okay?"

Kar chuckled. "At least once per meeting, Master Trey."

His companion laughed a good-natured laugh. "So tell me, Kar." Trey set his glass aside. "Before you give me the bloody details. Why do you want to help this guy? I'm curious."

Kar considered his answer well before giving it. "It fascinates me. Perhaps in some of the same ways the King was and is, fascinated by your situation."

The mortal let out another laugh. "Does that include flirting with him the way Michel did me?"

Kar offered up a smile. "I don't know about that. More importantly, he came looking for me. Most importantly, he managed to *find* me, which is interesting enough on its own, but…I feel it also deserves some reward. The end of a quest. And I don't at all believe that he wants to be a killer, Trey."

Trey made himself comfortable on his sofa, nodding all the while. "Yeah…yeah, he does deserve something, then. All right, I think you need to tell me this story from the beginning. 'Cause now I'm super curious. If you have time, I mean."

Kar settled across from the young man on the other peach colored sofa, and began his tale.

**

Viktor sat in a dark, quiet corner of the nondescript bar he'd found within walking distance of their hotel. It was a bit of a dive, being on the outskirts as it was. Only three miles or so from *The Fall Out*.

But *The Fall Out* wasn't a place for quiet, contemplative drinking, so that had been out of the question. Besides which, he was worried he might meet another…Cold woman.

He'd been nursing his fourth Chivas for a few minutes, now. Contemplating the morning's coffee date with Mitch and Damona. He'd shown up at their room twenty minutes after the encounter with Damona, the scent of coffee wafting out under the door to greet him. Disconcertingly, they'd acted as if everything were normal. Damona in particular was going out of her way to appear unconcerned, and even Mitch had noticed. By the vibe, Viktor guessed she hadn't mentioned word one about their encounter in Viktor's bedroom.

Having at first been intent on asking them what they'd talked about while he was absent, Viktor decided it was easier to go with the flow and let them have their fantasy of normalcy. Normal as defined by their group, anyway. In great part, it was in deference to the red haired vixen, the taste of whom coffee couldn't eradicate.

He knocked back the rest of his drink and motioned the barkeep for a refill. Viktor had copped out, and excused himself from breakfast, from any talk of sightseeing, or discussing, even, the business of being a band and the fact *The Fall Out* management had offered a very sweet deal.

Viktor couldn't spare the brain cells for that discussion, this morning. The deal would mean staying in one place longer than he found comfortable. It would mean being in that bar, surrounded by temptations and feelings the likes of which he'd never known. He remembered the darkness of the energy when they performed, dark and alluring, electric.

Different.

The barkeep poured two fingers. Viktor signaled for more. Double. Triple.

He ran his finger along the rim of the glass after the man left to tend other patrons, contemplating. He was certain Kar was the reason for the offer of a long-term gig. Kar was going to help him. It made sense they should have something to do while hanging around the area. They could make money while Viktor followed a lead on his personal life.

But Viktor was considering that maybe he should bag the whole thing, and take off. Alone. It was time. He'd gone too far with Damona. He was going to hurt her physically, not just emotionally, next time. He just knew it.

Feared it.

He sipped his drink

Mitch wouldn't understand. He was like the little brother, who no matter what, looked up to him in some way. Followed him around. Mitch didn't have anyone else. He knew that. He didn't want to abandon him.

Them.

But he had to. It was for the best. It was better for him, too. Seeing Damona every day, but not having her? He was about to explode. He could be a very patient man, but it was beyond all sanity, now.

"Bring him the bottle."

Viktor looked up from the bills the owner of the voice had dropped on the counter, and into the face of a rather hand-some – very handsome, he decided – young male.

**

"He did what?"

Damona fanned the air. "You heard me. What should we do? He needs our help."

Mitch paced and drew deeply of his clove.

"He, he…make him see a doctor?"

Mitch stopped pacing and gaped at her. "Like, have him committed?"

Damona's expression suggested he'd just told her to sacrifice her first-born child. "No, stupid! Just…just I think he needs…augh! I don't know. Maybe there is a tumor or something." Her hand came to her mouth after speaking the unthinkable. It dropped with little ceremony. "I've heard such things make people behave strange."

Mitch threw his smoke down and smeared it with his heel. "No, no, that can't be it, no way."

"You think I want it to be so? You prefer he's crazy?"

Mitch stopped walking and looked at her. He wilted like warm lettuce. "No. Of course not. I don't want him to die, either." Though Mitch wondered that Viktor wouldn't die any-way, if he kept up with certain things. "Where did he go?"

"You know as well as me." Damona dug around in her bag until she found her own cancer stick to light.

"We shoulda kept him here."

Damona's laugh was harsh. "But of course, because he's so easy to stop."

Mitch picked at his nails, while trying to think of some-thing to say. Something less hopeless sounding.

"I think he went to some bar," Damona said, smoke littering her words.

"That narrows it down."

"Fuck you, too."

Mitch looked up from his shoes to see Damona's sour – and hurt –expression. She had one arm across her body, and she rested her other elbow on its wrist, which kept the Lucky near her mouth at all times, this way.

"I'm sorry," he said. "I know you're worried. Really worried, because otherwise, you wouldn't have said shit to me about what happened in his room." He sighed and shoved his hands deep into his pockets. "So that freaks me out, because you never tell me shit like that."

A piece of tobacco stuck to Damona's tongue. Rather than pick it off, she spit. It took three tries.

Mitch looked away. He wasn't offended. He just knew it meant she had no other response.

**

The male Viktor scrutinized stirred something within him, something deep and forbidden. The large blue eyes, the full mouth, the luxurious hair, the strong, symmetrical bone structure of his face. But it was more than outward beauty. The stranger had a vibe that fingered dark places in strange and delightful ways.

"Thank you for the gesture," Viktor said, "and I must say, you're very pretty, but I'm –"

"Trey. Kar sent me." The stranger offered his hand.

Viktor just kept the surprise from registering on his face. "Sent you?" Sent him for what, he had to wonder.

"Yeah, well. He told me I could find you here."

Viktor gazed at Trey a moment, and at last took his hand. He noted the man's handshake was firm, confident.

"Another glass?" The barkeep said as he set the bottle down. Trey gave a nod, and said glass appeared shortly after.

He picked up the Chivas and poured each of them a healthy dose of it, then raised his glass. "To solving a mystery."

Viktor studied the man yet again. The deep blue eyes, deep and blue as the Aegean Sea. Something about them...

Viktor lifted his glass. "As you say." He had a sense that the other man didn't travel alone. Even when there was no other physically present.

Trey chuckled and downed his drink in one fluid swallow. He poured himself another, and studied Viktor in return. "Funny."

"What is?"

"You don't look possessed." His full lips quirked and he tossed a wink.

Viktor sharpened a brow. "Possessed? Is that what...is that what Kar thinks?" Viktor also wondered how this man would know, but one question at a time.

"He doesn't know for sure. That's why he came to me," Trey said.

"You have knowledge of such things?"

The other man's lips curved, conveying some *inside* knowledge, or joke, of some sort.

Viktor arched a brow, curious, but with nothing to say in the face of Trey's expression.

"Yeah," Trey said, at last. "You could say I do. But let's not discuss it in here."

Viktor's eyes bounced between the other man's, and he shrugged. "Very well. Lead on."

His companion latched onto the bottle as he came off the barstool. "This way."

Viktor slid off his stool and followed.

13

He sat in the passenger seat of the copper Murciélago. Another time, Viktor might have paused to study the lush interior of the Lamborghini, which he knew upon a cursory glance, was pristine. The sweetness of the exterior wasn't lost on him, either, when he was stepping inside.

But his focus was on the young lawyer in the driver's seat. That's what Mr. du Bois had told him on the way to the car. That he was a lawyer, representing some important people.

"So lawyers do well in Paris, I see. Or just you?"

Trey capped the bottle and set it in the back, all the while grinning at Viktor.

"It was a gift," he said. "From my bosses. So yes, I do well."

"You have generous…bosses."

The lawyer laughed. "It's best to be on their good side."

Viktor studied Trey, as if he could see the meaning behind the words, there in his eyes.

Those eyes were smiling, a spark in their depths.

"Kar gave me the details you offered him," Trey said, flipping a switch and becoming serious. Business-like. "I'd like to know if there's more. I can't help you if you aren't forthcoming."

The man was very direct. Viktor appreciated it, where others might bristle. He conjured a smile. "I didn't leave anything out when I spoke to Kar, so if he told you everything…"

"I think you did. Leave something out, that is."

Viktor's eyes narrowed. "You're calling me a liar?"

Trey's mouth tilted. "Do you know another word for it?" He held up a hand. "Listen. I'm not trying to start a fight. But I'm real good at reading people." He turned in his seat and made a bold lean in Viktor's direction. "Also, you look like a cross between an old fashioned cinema vampire and a zombie. What's fascinating is that it's not intentional. No make-up. I'm thinking you haven't seen a good sleep in…oh… years? Not that you aren't nice looking. You just don't appear healthy."

Viktor blinked – a jerky movement that made his entire face twitch. He was surprised. How accurate it was. Also, by the other man's wording.

Cinema vampire? Why not simply vampire? Why that word at all?

"Vampire?" Viktor said aloud, and to his amazement, Trey offered him a knowing look and smile.

"You're in denial?" Trey said, then seemed to think better of it, and shook his head. "No. You know what he is. That he's not the only one. I know how he found you." Amusement made itself known in his laugh. "And I thought my introductions were wild. You got me beat." He leaned back. "You can say it, Viktor, it's all right."

"Then he is what I think he is."

Trey offered a slow nod. "Though you should broaden that to they. What you thought *they* were, and are."

Viktor sat in silence, contemplating those words.

"I work for vampires, dude." Trey said, then. "You get used to it. Even learn to like it. I do, anyway."

"Who are these vampires?" It was now Viktor who leaned.

"For now, let's just say they're very, very important when it comes to non-humans. Kar works for them, too."

Viktor's brows rose. "And he sent you to help me." He looked at Trey with fresh eyes. "Why you? What's special about you? There must be something?"

A burst of raucous laughter filled the car's interior. "Oh, the ways I could answer that," Trey replied. "There's something, all right."

Viktor relaxed and joined in the laughter, albeit more subdued. There was certainly something. A charisma, a strange charm, which was good, otherwise, Viktor could imagine Trey garnering a few slaps (and punches) in his lifetime.

"You're an interesting man, Trey."

"I know."

"And cocky."

"It's not cocky if it's true."

Viktor smiled.

"So, then. Fill me in on the rest, Viktor. I want to help you."

Viktor settled back, and tried to gather the words to explain the unexplainable.

**

Damona walked back and forth, scraping a drumstick across the bricks of the wall as she did, much to the consternation of a man sitting not far away on a bench. Not that she noticed. Nor did she notice that the stick was splintering, because it had absorbed all of her tension for the last few minutes.

They'd gone into Paris. Mitch's idea. But she'd grown tired of sitting at the bistro, and stalked off, threatening to yank off his scrotum if he followed her.

Damona took her need for solace quite seriously.

She'd wandered until finding herself inside the walls of Père Lachaise. She had no idea what tombs were close by, nor did she care. She just kept pacing, pacing, until the man on the bench gave up, and left in search of another bench.

Not that she noticed.

Damona couldn't decide what to do. Someone at *The Fall Out* had contacted them just before they'd driven into Paris. This someone wanted to know if they were still considering the offer. An offer she knew nothing about, but pretended to. Told the man that yes, they were discussing it.

Viktor hadn't told them about this offer, and Damona wanted to know why. She was having thoughts she didn't like. Fears. She was worried that Viktor was going to do something rash. Like leave. For her own good. He thought she didn't know. That she never suspected. Or maybe he did; he knew that she was perceptive.

He hadn't left, not yet, but she just knew that events in his room had caused him to reconsider. She just knew that he was going to disappear, leave her behind.

It made her angry. And sad. Afraid.

She dropped her drumstick, giving it a reprieve, and reached into her purse. Her fingers contacted her cell. She thought to call him, but he hadn't answered the other two times, and she didn't want to seem needy or desperate.

Or worried.

She let out a sound of anguish, her hands to her face. She should just tell him. Tell him that she loved him. That she wanted him. Though if he didn't already know, he was an idiot, she thought. But she should say it. What was the harm in saying it? Why hesitate? She might not ever get the chance again.

She lowered her hands. Yes, she should tell him before he went away and she never saw him again. There were unspoken words between her and her family. The war of independence in her country had robbed her of so many moments. Her chance to tell them how much she loved them.

She couldn't let this happen again. She couldn't, she just couldn't. She'd closed up, to protect herself, but Viktor had still seeped into her, against her will, and she couldn't take it any longer. Let him all the way in, she had to let him in, invite him blunt and plain. He might refuse, but she realized that she had no choice. She had to know. Now, or never.

She pulled out the phone and tried, once more, to get in contact with Viktor. This time, she'd leave a message if he didn't answer. She couldn't have him taking off without at least a message.

**

Trey leaned back in his seat after Viktor finished his story. "I'm gonna need to watch you sleep. That's all there is to it."

Viktor studied the other man. "Watch me sleep…"

The lawyer arched a brow. "As handsome as you are, I'm not being a pervert."

Viktor couldn't help a chuckle. "I didn't think you were."

"Clearly, you need to get to know me better, because I totally am." Trey grinned, but then waved a hand. "Really. It might help if I see this for myself. What you're like when you wake up from one of these nightmares, and whether you do anything during a nightmare. Maybe you really are sleepwalking."

"I've considered that, but it seems…different."

"How would you know?"

Viktor gave a slight nod. "Good point. Then again, I told you Mitch saw me kill someone wide-awake. So to speak."

"Well, it's starting point."

"How will you know if I'm really asleep, or faking, or just insane?"

Trey shrugged. "Maybe I won't. But I can't say, until I see for myself." He reached into the back for the bottle of Chivas.

"It's not safe." Viktor took the offered bottle. "I've killed people."

"Kar can be with me, if it makes you feel better."

"But I've killed them, too."

"Them?" Trey chuckled. "Come on, now."

"I've killed *vampires*." Viktor's fingers worried the bottle's cap.

Trey arched a brow at the other man. "Neither of us is going to be fucking you, so I think we'll be fine."

Viktor's eyes dropped to the bottle.

"I'm sorry, that was harsh. But that's when it happened. Why mince words? You're not a man of delicacies, from what I can tell," Trey said.

Viktor shook his head and removed the cap from the bottle. He brought it to his lips and had a healthy swig. "But that man I killed. He wasn't fucking me, either." He followed that with a longer drink. "I can't think why you'd want to help me."

Trey read his companion's expression, his demeanor, and read them well. "I can see that it haunts you. So clearly, Kar was right; you're not a psychopath. If there's something driving you to violence that can be fixed, I want to find it. If it's in my realm of expertise, that is." He shrugged. "Let's just say I'm accustomed to what others consider abnormal." After a short pause, he added, "And honestly? It's perversely fascinating." He winked. "I'm into that, too."

Viktor toyed with the cap for a time, before replying. He'd not confessed so much, before. He felt naked in a very different way.

"What would that be? Your area of expertise?" Viktor asked.

"Hah. That might take while to explain. Before we get to the subject of me, there's something else I'm wondering about you."

Viktor lifted his gaze and found the other man's face.

"Why haven't you ever sought help from a doctor? A psychiatrist or something? Anything?" Trey asked.

"They might lock me up. Fill me with drugs." Yet another drink did Viktor take.

"If you're so concerned about the safety of others around you, wouldn't that be the best choice?"

Viktor looked the other man dead in the eyes. Unflinching.

"Yes," he said. "I can't explain it properly. I know it doesn't make sense, because I *do* care. But I can't be locked up, I just can't. Part of me...I tried, once." He capped the liquor bottle. "I tried to walk into a doctor's office."

Trey merely gazed at him, waiting for the words he knew were yet to come.

"I had an episode, as I sometimes call them."

Trey spread his hands. "Let me guess. You killed the doctor?"

Viktor shook his head and set the bottle in the floorboard at his feet. He lifted his shirt to reveal his taut stomach. Trey watched, a question sitting in his eyes.

"See the circular scar?"

Trey nodded. There were a few scars, but one was indeed circular, and very close to his navel.

"It seems I did it to myself," Viktor said.

"When you tried to go to the doctor?"

The brunet lowered his shirt. "Yes."

Trey's head tilted. "You stabbed yourself?"

"With a screwdriver I must have found lying about. No one else was around. It got my attention."

Trey's brows lifted. "So it – something – stopped you? With force? Is that what you're saying? Because that can happen with possession."

"I don't know what I'm saying, Trey." Viktor reached for the bottle. "I can tell you I get ill at the thought of submitting myself to testing. Literally ill." He tapped the side of the bottle, in thought. "And I don't mind admitting that it frightens me. I don't know what they'd do. Probably lobotomize me. I'd rather die."

Trey's eyes moved over Viktor. He didn't tell him that he thought lobotomies were mostly in the past. In some countries. That wasn't the point. He remained silent a time, content to study the other man, and contemplate what he'd learned of Viktor so far. He wasn't sensing a spirit within Viktor just now, but they could come and go.

He was the first to break the silence, for all his scrutiny.

"Well," Trey said. "You seem to mean that. Hence the scar, perhaps." He contemplated that in some way, Viktor was seeking assisted suicide, messing with vampires as he did.

Viktor ran his fingers over the bottle's label. He could feel his cell vibrating in his pocket. Now wasn't the time to answer it, and so he did his best to ignore it. He was confident he knew who it was, anyway.

"Should we shoot for tonight, or are you going to drink yourself into oblivion?" Trey said.

Viktor shook his head. "The sooner the better." He lifted his gaze to the man in the other seat. "But tell me something. What do you know about possession?"

"I know plenty. I might tell you more later, but for now, that'll have to do. Just know Kar wouldn't ask me for this favor if I wasn't up to the task. Will that do for the time being?"

Viktor studied the other man with fresh curiosity. "Yes, I suppose it will have to do. It certainly can't hurt and I doubt anyone else would help me."

Trey nodded. "Need a ride somewhere?"

Viktor shook his head again and looked out the side window.

"Let me rephrase. Where can I drop you? Then I'll know where to find you, later. Unless you'd like to do it somewhere else."

Viktor's eyes shot to the other man. "Not there."

Trey shifted in his seat, fished the keys from his pocket, and started the car. It purred, powerfully, into life.

"We'll suss it out on the way," he said.

14

There was a knock. Viktor roused himself from the chair by the window, crossed the room, and opened the door. He already knew whom he'd find on the other side. He'd listened to Damona's message after Mr. du Bois dropped him off at the hotel, and he'd waited. Almost two hours, he'd waited, for the redhead to return from the city.

And there she was. Wide eyes met his, as if she were surprised to find him there. She was. He hadn't returned her call. Hadn't even texted her. But the first thing she did when arriving at the hotel, was go to his door.

Viktor had known she would. A gut instinct.

"Hi," she managed to say.

"Hi." His gaze swept over her, which left her feeling several things. He stepped back, giving her room to enter.

"Have a good time in Paris?" Viktor asked after she was inside, and he closed the door.

Damona considered. "Okay, I guess." She sat on the edge of the narrow bed and looked up at him. She made a confession. One to make up for the confession not quite made on the phone. "It would have been more fun with you."

Viktor laughed. The sound was flat. "Me? Fun?" Her voicemail ran through his mind, replayed, for the fifteenth time. He heard between the lines, the words she hadn't said.

But then he'd known what she wasn't saying for a long time, now.

"Yes, you," she replied. "Fun."

Viktor shrugged. "I didn't think of it as a word that suited me, before."

"Because you're so serious lately." She folded her arms.

"Lately?" He worked up a chuckle, though it felt insincere. He knew she wasn't in his room for small talk. He wondered if today was the day she'd say how she felt. Really felt.

"Viktor," she lowered her arms and stood up, "we can get help for you. I will…I will take care of you, not leave you, I –"

"Damona –"

"No, listen, listen, it will be okay, I'm sure it's a simple thing, hmm? There are good doctors right here, France…" she took a step towards him, taking a moment to gather more words. She'd never pushed, never pried, but now it was different. Now she felt some desperation, she felt as if time were running out.

Viktor held up his hands. "Damona, you don't understand. I was going to tell you before –"

"Please, Viktor I…I…love you."

"You love a killer!" The words escaped him the moment her declaration struck his heart. He knew. He had known for some time. But to hear her say it, this was all together different. As much as it touched him, it terrified him, too.

She gazed at him, her expression curiously unreadable. He wondered that she was in shock. He'd thought Mitch had told her what he'd seen. Maybe it was the same as her words to him. All together different hearing the killer confess it.

"You need to get away from me," Viktor said. "Do you understand? Don't love me. You should hate me."

She began to shake her head. "I knew it. You were going to leave, huh? Leave us. You're still going to leave. Why did you wait?"

He thought of Trey, of how Kar was trying to help him. But Viktor wasn't putting much faith in any of it. They may mean well, but somehow, he didn't think that whatever ailed him was curable. He didn't allow himself to hope that he could have the woman who smelled so good he could taste her from across the room.

"I can't stay with the two of you any longer," Viktor said. "I should've gone a year ago, at least."

Her chin lifted, defiant. "I came back before you could go, huh? Or did you wait? You didn't answer me."

He studied her. "That's it. Hate me, Damona. I need you to hate me."

"Rrrh!" She rushed at him and beat at his chest. "You're so stupid, stupid, stupid!" He didn't budge as she punctuated each word with a small fist. "I can't hate you! You think I didn't try!"

"Damona…"

"This is why you waited? To make me hate you? Why not just leave!" Her voice was so close to cracking, but helpless against her iron will. She was determined not to fall apart in front of him. Not completely.

He grabbed hold of her wrists. "I have to leave you precisely *because* I love you too, damn it."

Her eyes widened a touch. Her pupils grew. She stopped struggling.

Viktor's own eyes glossed. "Yes, I love you. And I'll love you to death if I don't leave."

She had no words in response. She didn't quite understand, or want to. She only knew that he'd finally said it. What she'd hoped for so long that he felt. That it wasn't her imagination. *I love you.* Those words weren't supposed to be a goodbye. They were meant for happy ever after – or the beginning of something beautiful.

"I don't want to hurt you, Damona. I already have, I know. But those wounds can heal."

There was a scant shake of her head. "You really do think you're dangerous to me," she whispered. "You really do. You're really going to leave me?"

He let go of her pale wrists and backed away. "It started when I was eleven. I think…" He turned away and moved, placing distance between them, distance he desperately needed. Once he reached the small bedside table, he turned to face her.

"Some other boys decided they needed to assert themselves over the outcast," he said. "I didn't have a Father that they knew. He didn't give me a name. He wasn't there when I was born. Mother wasn't married to him, and they knew he wasn't of our little clan. All strikes against her, us. I was outcast in the womb." He shrugged. "We moved on the outskirts of the group, sometimes. Well, these boys were tired of it, and one day, tied me up. Whipped me."

Damona's gaze wavered. She'd seen his scars. She knew the ones on his back well. He wasn't one to hide them. He wasn't shy, even if he wouldn't bed her. Her fingers drifted to her lips as it became clear where those had come from. But Viktor was still talking.

"Next I knew, some adult was dragging me away, and one boy was nearly dead, the other hurt badly. Or maybe he did die, I don't know. I struggled, somehow got away. Ran. Mother told me to run."

"I…they were hurting you, so…" Damona took a breath and began again. "If you're set to convince me this makes you bad, I don't understand. They were hurting you, and you defend yourself."

"The problem is that I don't remember attacking them, Damona." He spread his hands. "I don't know how I got free, or where I got the machete that I tried to gut one with. Just like I don't know what I did to that man Mitch saw me kill. I had to make him tell me."

He could see in her eyes that she knew. That Mitch had told her. But not the details. He was certain that Mitch was good enough to spare her the details.

"I don't know if he gave you the same excuses that he uses to convince himself he's right to stick with me," Viktor said, "but if he knew about the rest, I'm pretty sure even *he* would rethink his position. Loyalty is admirable. Until it becomes dangerous and stupid."

Damona was afraid to ask. She stood, paralyzed, not wishing to hear more, but unable to leave. He'd started his confession, things he'd never told her. She would bear witness. She had no choice. He told her that story for a reason, there had to be more.

"I've killed lovers," he said. He felt somewhat numb, now. The way she was looking at him, the words hanging cold and stark in the air, the knowledge he may never see her again after this night; it was a raw and ugly place. A lonely place.

So he went numb.

"One I cared for in a short time," he said. "Her name was Sylvan. The other, I didn't even know her name."

The slightest intake of air made the slightest sound in her throat. Her words, a bare slip of sound. "The woman…"

"From the *Fall Out*." Viktor held out his hands, palms up. "I've very fresh blood on these hands, darling."

The drummer took an involuntary step back. Another, which turned her in the direction of the door.

"There is something horribly wrong with me, Damona, and I don't want your blood on my hands. Actually…I do, but not that way."

He was numb, and now that he'd begun, perhaps a little too honest for her taste. She took another couple of steps, unshed tears quivering in the rims of her eyes, threatening to drip, drop.

"You'll do what you need to do," he told her. "And that's okay. But know that if you call the authorities, I'll be dead before they get through that door."

She froze.

"I won't go quietly," Viktor said. "I don't want to be someone's experiment. I don't want to be insane and drugged into nonexistence. I don't want to be studied, and I won't go to some prison where I'll find a way to kill other prisoners. I'll do what I should've done years ago. I'll kill *myself*." If he could. He wasn't certain that he could do even that.

Her tears fell, then. Diamonds that shined brighter than any he'd ever seen, glass sharp enough to cut right through him, and he would never forget. She fumbled with the door handle, and once getting purchase, threw open the door and fled the room.

It was then Viktor regained all of his feeling, a bright flare of pain and anguish that buckled his knees and introduced him to the floor.

15

Urgency. The press.
The press.
Anarchy.
Surrounded.
Still not afraid.

Some are shields, some are enemies, but indiscriminate,
death does not care.

Survival and retribution have no conscience.

Stone and candle, winding hall and furs.
Smell of roasted animal.

Master, Master come quick!

Woman, weeping. Weeping and afraid.
Pursued down a corridor, dark corridor.

An ill feeling begins to rise in the red clothed chest of the
one holding the serpentine sword.
Closer, closer. It rises, rises, until it is like bile in the
throat, wanting to choke breath, the taste putrid.

Chased by a sudden, near paralyzing fear.

Feet move automatically, leading into the large room. The room of silks, furs, fire blazing in the hearth, scent of smoke so sweet.
Silks many shades of red, silks golden, velvet crushed, some stained with blood most personal and other fluids.

Sanctuary, always it was sanctuary. Moments of purest peace, the only moments. Whispered words and sighs.

Understanding.
Light.
The brightest flame in a dark world.

Panic. Panic as footsteps lead to the tower window.

Someone is speaking, but words are lost. Eyes drift to the river below, loathe to look but compelled.

Rocks. A broken body.
A beautiful, now unnaturally pale-skinned body, dark hair billowing out, leaving snaking trails through the water. It could have been beautiful in a painting.

But this was real, far too real.

So real, her name cannot even be screamed. A Master goes to his knees, chest seized, heart wishing to stop, air lost.

Voices, voices. Wailing women, fearful women.
Servants.

Servants, yes.

Something in the mind shifts.
To die, lest be caught. To die, lest be parted forever.

Something else shifts.

The body rises from the broken kneel, sword swinging in the outstretched hand.

"You punish her, to punish me? You take everything, everything! This was not to be the price!

I CURSE you, I CURSE you, I CURSE YOU!"

The wail would bring tears to anyone's eyes.
The broken wail.

The screams of the women fall on distant ears, move nothing resembling sympathy, nothing at all.

The human heart, soul, weeps and wails.

The rest is blank.

Blood spatters, women and men alike scream. All will pay the price, all will pay.

"Master, we must flee!"

The words and cries are soon gurgles being spat up with liquid over his chin as he is slowly disemboweled where he stands.

"YOU FAILED ME! YOU FAILED HER!"

Death. Death might be welcome, now, vision is going black.

"It is not time for you to die."

"CURSE YOU!"

But the words are wept.

He is carried along with those that escaped the slash, the stab, the finality of metal, brutal grief and anger.

Secret winding passages.
Tunnels.

Carried along on feet that have no will of their own. Carried along, spirit broken for now.

When the name can be uttered, near silently, it becomes a babbling thing, an incoherent thing. It is the only thing the Master can or will say for hours and hours and hours.

They are more fearful of him than ever in this display of hopelessness and despair.

This...weakness.

Fearful for him, even, for this monster, as they have never seen him this way. The iron fist, reduced to a helpless puddle of liquid.

Some even manage sympathy.

But fear is never far, because they know when the liquid becomes solid once more...

All will pay in ways best not imagined.
Even their worst nightmares will not compare.

16

"Kar!"

"Stay back, Master Trey." The Asian shoved him back even farther with his free hand. With his other hand, he grasped the blade that had buried itself in his useless intestines and even now, threatened to twist.

It had impaled him when he stepped between Viktor and Trey, just as the former had lunged. He could have stopped it, perhaps. He hadn't wished to do that, for more than one reason. A different instinct had told him that he shouldn't interrupt whatever was happening. That he should let it play out.

Viktor had had a nightmare, or so they'd thought. They'd witnessed what appeared to be a man dreaming an intense scene, or alternate reality. Trey had been watching too closely. Viktor had begun to rant and wail. To curse in a language neither of them clearly understood, they only knew it sounded like several oaths.

The young lawyer cum medium had moved even closer, to hear some of the whispered words that followed, see if he could make them out, and to make sure they recorded well.

That's when Viktor had leaped from the bed, nearly knocking Trey off the edge, and moved across the room. Trey had followed, as Viktor was screaming at the walls, in that same language.

Mr. du Bois hadn't seen the Rom reach into the black boot and pull out the serrated blade.

But Kar had.

The vampire could perhaps have knocked the blade away, or engaged the human. But there was a second reason he didn't. Though baser instincts would have had him hurt the human, even kill him for the threat, another part of him resisted. He didn't want to hurt him. Or kill him. He merely wished to protect Trey.

That's why he was present, after all. That, and to aid in the diagnoses.

Kar stood there, skewered, blood dripping from his palm to run down the steel that bit into it. He was curious if this waking dream, or whatever it was, would run a course. Come to some conclusion.

He stared into Viktor's (or not Viktor's, he was not certain) piercing grey eyes, and listened as the other man queried. He didn't understand, but he could tell that there were questions. That the human was asking him – or someone in the dream – questions.

Kar began to think the language vaguely familiar, but Viktor was too agitated, it flowed too fast. Since he couldn't speak it, he chose the first that came to mind.

"I do not know," Kar said in Russian.

"Who sent the letter?"

Kar's brows rose. Viktor had understood and replied in kind.

"What letter?"

Steel attempted once again to twist his insides. Kar couldn't stay the growl. Somewhere behind him, Trey made a sound, and it drew Viktor's attention, attention Kar promptly reclaimed.

"What letter?" Kar asked once more.

"Who told her that I was dead?"

The Asian was searching for a proper reply when Viktor let out a wail. And another, that formed a name. Grey eyes then widened in horror, even as a veil seemed to part in their depths, and he stumbled back.

"Kar?"

The vampire began the task of extricating steel from flesh. "Yes. Viktor?" His dark gaze remained fixed on the other man. He'd seen someone else in the mortal's eyes. Something else.

"I…" the human didn't seem certain. "Yes. Viktor." His gaze dropped to Kar's bloodstained shirt. "Oh God."

"I'll heal."

Behind him, Trey let out a puff of air and shut off the recorder. "Dudes, that was, sorry to use the term, gnarly."

Viktor got a good look at the American. "Are you hurt? Did I hurt you, too?"

Trey shook his head. "No. Kar took the hit. Don't worry, I've seen worse. He'll be okay." He shrugged. "But if you do that again, I might need to deck you."

Viktor covered his face with his hands. "Fuck. Just kill me now. Just…fuck."

"Okay, too soon for levity," Trey said. "Listen. You didn't mean to do it. It wasn't you."

Viktor's hands dropped. "So I'm possessed? Is this where you perform an exorcism?"

The tiny spark of hope in Viktor's eyes made it difficult for Trey to speak his next words. "I…don't think you're possessed. It may look like it, but it doesn't feel quite the same."

Viktor sagged. Kar remained silent. Healed, and holding the knife.

"Are you sure?" Viktor asked, though he knew the answer.

"There's no one for me to connect to," Trey said. "What I mean is that I would be able to sense the spirit. Speak to it."

"Cross the veil…"

"Not all the way. But yes. I have a foot on the Other Side."

"Wait. If some spirit was in me –"

Trey held up a hand. "I know what you're thinking. Let me clarify. I could force it to speak to me."

Viktor's brows knit. "How?"

Trey handed him a patient look. "You might better ask why. But now isn't the time."

Viktor thought it might very well be the time, but relented, too freshly scattered to press. He turned away and moved towards the bed. "Seriously, kill me. Be done with it. Kar can do it."

"Who said that Kar wanted to?" Trey said.

"No one. You have not given him time to assess the situation, Viktor," Kar said. "He did say that it wasn't you. It may not be possession, but there are other options."

Viktor turned back. "Like what? Chemical imbalance? Back to being insane."

Trey broke in before Kar could respond.

"I said it wasn't you. You didn't seem to be in control, but in a way that…" Trey spread his arms. "Doesn't happen often, but I'm lost for words. It *did* feel like you weren't in control, due to some other force."

"But I'm not possessed. What am I, then?" Viktor's gaze spoke to his building confusion.

Trey moved towards him. "Do you speak something resembling…Turkish, maybe?"

Viktor shook his head. He wondered why Trey hadn't answered his question. "Why ask me that?"

"What languages do you speak?" Trey pressed.

"A little French, some Hungarian. A word or three of Romanian. Very bad Romanian." He shook his head. "I don't understand. What are you getting at?"

Kar noted that Viktor did not mention Russian.

"Ah," Trey pointed at him. "Romanian. Interesting. But you're not fluent?"

"No. I never have been. My mother knew a few words, but we never really spoke it. She preferred Hungarian." She'd said his father was Hungarian.

Trey pressed a button on his digital recorder. Then another. A voice issued from the device, and Viktor was more confused than ever. He didn't know this voice, and he didn't grasp the language.

Trey said, "It's you. Speaking what might be a form of Romanian, but I'm not sure. Doesn't happen to be one of the languages I know."

Viktor's dark brows shot up then furrowed anew. They rose once again when his cry of *Elisabetha* filled the room.

Silence followed. Trey had turned off the recording.

17

"I'm not possessed, but I'm speaking in tongues?"

Viktor sat heavily on the end of the bed. He'd refused to get his hopes up, but the way he was feeling suggested hope had wormed its way into him, nonetheless.

Trey held up his hands. "Well. Unless you're possessed by something I haven't met before."

Viktor arched a brow at him. "Like what? A demon? Comforting thought."

Kar drifted towards the door and stilled, as if he were standing guard and bearing witness at the same time.

Trey's tone was sympathetic. "Sorry. I need to do some research." Such as asking a special friend or two if they knew the language on the recording. If they could translate it.

Viktor sighed. "And prolong the inevitable?"

"You're getting more nihilistic by the second," Trey said. "Did you think this could be fixed like that?" He snapped his fingers.

Viktor's gaze dropped. "No. Of course not."

"You didn't strike me as the type to give up so easily." Trey moved closer.

"Hah! You know how many *years* I've gone on like this." Viktor's eyes flashed old resentments.

Trey's expression softened. "I know it's been several. I think you're really fucking tired, all the way to your soul. I get it, really I do. Much as I can, not being you." He began to reach for the other man, and stopped himself at the last second. "But why give in now, when I might find a real lead?"

Viktor studied and studied him. His posture relaxed. "Fair point. I've never had so much as a sliver of a lead."

"So give me a little time, Viktor. It's not like you need to be somewhere." Trey touched his shoulder. "Do you?"

Viktor made no reply. He needed to be *away*. Anywhere that Mitch and Damona, weren't. After that, he did not know.

Start over? No. He'd had enough transitory friends, he decided. One sometimes got weary, pretending to be made of iron. Of maintaining brick walls, sealing every crack, mixing new mortar.

Perhaps it was time to grab Death by the balls.

Lines creased Trey's face as he watched Viktor. "Give me a chance. Just one chance. All right? If I fail," he glanced at Kar, who nodded, "I will see to it that your wishes are carried out."

Viktor studied the flooring. The thought of suicide was a strange one, foreign to him. Yes, he'd placed himself in situations that were dangerous. Seeking, perhaps, assisted suicide. Yet he'd never really thought of it in those terms. Death was after him and he didn't want to wait for it, cowering in some corner. He was going to meet it head on.

Had that simply been a way to make it sound nobler? Less of a defeat, surrender? Trey was right. He was soul tired. That the other man could see so much, made him a bit uncomfortable.

He pushed his hair back and lifted his eyes to Trey. "All right. A little more time."

The other man nodded.

Viktor thought of Mitch. Damona. Mostly Damona. He wondered where she'd gone, if she was at the hotel. If she was coming back. He knew it would be better if she didn't, but that didn't stop him from wanting to see her face. Hear her husky, Croatian accented voice, calling from the door. *Coffee?*

He snapped out of his reverie when he realized Trey had asked him a question, and was waiting for him to answer.

"I'm sorry," Viktor said. "What was that?"

"Do you know much of your ancestry?"

The question caught Viktor off guard in a way it never had, before. He'd always avoided most conversations that dealt with family. He'd found it easy to deflect, distract. As he looked into those dark blue eyes, he found his throat closing around a lump.

Viktor decided he must be very, very tired, to be so susceptible to all of these feelings. If he said that aloud, he had no doubt Trey would laugh, or tell him that he was stating the obvious. Someone who forced himself into a life of insomnia, tired? A colossal understatement. Yet Viktor had gotten used to it, as many do. Perhaps eased along by the fact that he wasn't searching for a sleeping potion. He was finding new ways to stake awake.

Or maybe he was just living in a constant dream-like state. Sometimes he wondered, when he actually stopped to think about it. A haze that had become normal. Just as people under pressure find it normal after a time, even think they do well under the circumstances.

A lie. When the stress was gone, they collapsed – a helpless mess.

He didn't want to wilt in this place at this time.

"Viktor?"

He rubbed his face. He understood that Trey wouldn't ask if he didn't have a reason. If it wasn't important to his situation. That much he could reason out.

"Did your father speak a few languages? Some you might have learned very young, but have forgotten, since you didn't use them?"

Viktor stared up at Trey. "I don't know. If you can find him, ask him."

Trey's lips parted, but no words followed.

"I don't know his name; I don't know who he is, or where he is. I never did," Viktor said. "Just that he spoke Hungarian." That and a ridiculous story his mother used to tell him. She knew it would amuse him at the time. He doubted it was true, so it didn't seem important enough to share.

Trey offered a slight nod. "Mother?"

"Mother is dead."

Trey looked at Kar. The vampire knew what Trey was considering. Neither spoke the thought aloud.

"You think you can speak to her," Viktor said for them. He spread his hands when the other human's eyes widened. "Don't look so surprised. You're some kind of medium, sensitive; I believe it and have not questioned you."

Trey's brows lifted. "You never did, no. About that…"

"I'm no stranger to what others deem silly superstitions. Frauds. But I don't think you can reach her any longer. I think she moved on."

Trey couldn't help but be curious. "Why do you think that?"

"Because I never sense her anymore."

The young lawyer saw Viktor in a brighter light. "I wondered about you. There was something more going on than bad dreams. And that discoloration in your iris. I've heard before that it's a sign of a seer in your culture. Superstition or not."

"My culture?" He laughed. "I suppose I had some, once." Viktor shrugged. "But yes, occasionally I see things. Sometimes these things come to pass."

Trey sat on the edge of the bed beside him, giving Viktor just enough personal space. "Have you seen anything lately?"

Viktor nodded.

"What was it?"

"Red hair spilled across a pillow, brighter than the blood spilled across the sheets."

Viktor was so certain that this was Damona, this vision he'd had not so long ago, that he'd all but chased her out of that hotel room. That vision had been the last push. It convinced him that he *had to leave*.

Trey was studying him when he looked in that direction. The man had seen Damona somewhere, he could tell. Read it on his face. The reaction to his words. He didn't need to tell Trey what the vision meant.

"Give me just a little time, Viktor," he said. "A day. Two."

Viktor turned his gaze to Kar. "Don't let me leave this place. Don't tell them where I am. Don't take me back." He shifted his gaze to Trey and back. "Don't. Even if I beg."

His Savior offered a slight bow of his head "As you wish." He would also make certain, from now on, that the Rom didn't have access to his blade. He'd known that Viktor could be dangerous, yet he'd been remiss in checking for the knife when he arrived. The two men were already in the townhouse, discussing things.

Kar was not normally remiss. It would not happen again. Because if Kar had been *forced* to make a choice, Viktor would be a corpse in need of disposal.

"We won't," Trey agreed. He turned his attention to Kar. "I think I'll go ask Michel if he knows the language Viktor was speaking. Or knows someone who does."

"He was yet in his office when I last checked in," Kar said.

Trey gave a nod and stood, touching Viktor's shoulder again along the way. "I'll be back."

The Rom watched him leave. He studied the Asian.

"Michel?" he asked.

"The king," Kar said.

Viktor contemplated this. "You have kings. I assume you mean of your kind, since France ousted its royalty."

"Yes."

Viktor left it at that and looked about the room. It was of a different time. What century, he wasn't certain. But older.

"This is one of his properties," Kar supplied.

The mortal returned to studying the vampire. "This doesn't surprise me. It's very nice." King. A powerful vampire, then? Or the cleverest of them.

"There is no need to entertain me with conversation, unless you yourself require it," Kar said.

Viktor laughed at that, there was no help for it. The wording, the directness. "Not if I'm going to bore you to tears."

"I don't know about that. But I am comfortable with silence, if you prefer. You may sleep, if you wish. I will watch over you."

Viktor gave a vigorous shake of his head. "I don't want to sleep. I don't…" he paused. He ran his fingers through his hair. "I don't want to be someone else. Whatever that means. When I'm awake, I'm myself. Some of the time." He let go with another laugh. A dry, humorless laugh. "Maybe I never knew who I was."

Kar contemplated this, observing the human for a moment.

"I will make you some strong coffee," he said.

"Oh no. You don't need to wait on me. I can do it."

"I really do not mind. I'm accustomed to serving." With that, he left the room.

And Viktor pondered his parting comment.

18

Mitch did another circuit of the hotel grounds, not that anything would change. Viktor still wouldn't be outside the lobby entrance. But it was better than wearing out the cheap carpet in the room he and Damona shared. A room she hadn't returned to any more than Viktor had returned to his. If Mitch thought they'd run off somewhere together and were finally consummating their unspoken relationship, he'd be raising a glass to their empty beds and not pacing.

He didn't think this was the case.

They were late. They were never late for gigs. They were supposed to play that club again, *Fall Out*. Unless he'd mixed up the dates, or heard Viktor wrong.

He reversed direction and started around the hotel again. He wasn't wrong. They had a gig. They were beyond late. He had called and called both Viktor and Damona, and neither had answered. They hadn't returned his texts, either. He rubbed his head, ruffling his hair, as the thought about the last time he saw either of them.

Viktor had slipped into a fancy looking car with a fancy looking dude. Mitch had glimpsed them when he exited the hotel, thinking to go find a drink, or simply take a walk, get some air. He'd stepped out just in time to see Viktor disappear inside the car, and watch it take off.

Fast.

Sweet ride, he'd thought at the time. Lucky Vik. It wasn't the first time he'd gone off with a man. Viktor had never hidden his preferences. It was something Mitch liked about him. He was who he was, and you could like it or leave it.

A fast car and a fit dude. Understandable that Viktor might not want to rush back to his cramped hotel room. Except that no matter how much fun Viktor was having, no matter how many times he could slip by them like a shadow and do whatever it was that he did, Viktor always returned for gigs.

It was not his way to be late. Mitch had often mused that Viktor had some internal setting, some silent alarm that went off when he was due at a club. Once or twice, Viktor had made them sweat by showing up at whatever bar they were playing at, instead of meeting up with them at the hotel. Or they'd go get him. But no matter what, he'd always been in time to help pack in.

Mitch was beginning to worry even more. He wanted his paycheck, sure, but they could get others. He worried something bad had happened. If not to Viktor – Mitch shivered at the thought – to the man with the sports car. He had seen Viktor gut someone. There was no denying that part of the memory. He'd performed a vivisection on a standing man. It hadn't registered, hadn't truly sunk in, until he and Mitch were fast and far away.

That's when Mitch had puked, and after that, had come to understand that Viktor appeared to have amnesia.

Where Damona fit into this, he didn't know. Maybe she didn't, but it couldn't be a coincidence, her being AWOL, as well. Or it could. But Mitch wasn't buying that.

Just when he was coming up with the worst possible scenario, a familiar scent came to him. Then the clack-clack of heels. He realized it had been longer since he'd seen *her,* than Viktor.

"Hey!" He broke into a trot, then a run, when he caught the flash of red hair by the entrance. "Damona! Wait up."

She kept right on going, into the hotel. *Fine*, he thought. He'd just have to corner her. He sped inside and caught her up.

"Hey," he grabbed her elbow. "Why didn't you stop? Where you been, anyway?"

She jerked her arm away and click-clacked towards the stairwell, opened the door, and headed up.

"What the – hey!" Mitch caught the door just before it caught him in the face, and followed. "Why are you ignoring me? Did I do something to you I don't remember doing? Or not do something you wanted me to do?"

No response. On she went, up the stairs, him trailing behind like a confused puppy with nowhere else to go.

"Damona, what happened? What's wrong? Is it Viktor?" Mitch was getting an indescribable feeling in the pit of his stomach.

"Arrrg!"

Mitch stopped. It wasn't a response he expected, or one he wanted. When he realized she had kept moving, and was exiting on the second floor, he ran up and followed her through the door.

"Viktor, Viktor, always Viktor," she muttered as she walked down the hall, her steps now muffled by flat carpet. "Bah!"

Mitch followed in silence. She was using words suggesting anger, but her tone didn't match. He could hear something else. Like hurt. Sadness.

Heartbreak? Did it make a sound like the wail she let out before?

"You know something?" she said. She stopped and turned so suddenly, Mitch almost walked into her. "Fuck Viktor, okay?"

She whirled back around and continued down the hall until she reached her door. Theirs, hers and Mitch's door. She was fighting with the lock when Mitch made his way to her.

"Um, D? It's the next room," he said.

"Fuck." She marched to the next hotel room door and let herself inside. Mitch, still the puppy, was hot on her heels.

He watched her proceed to tear the room apart. *Wow. That must have been some fight.*

She'd cool down, or so he hoped. "Why don't you take a breath, sit down, and tell me about it," he said.

She kept throwing her few belongings into her bag. Or at it. He could see how scattered she truly was, as she hadn't finished that when she went into the bathroom and with a sweep of her arm, scooped some things into her giant hand-bag. Many of which tumbled to the floor.

"Some of that…" *is mine*, he finished in his head, thinking it didn't need said, after all. But of course, she'd pick that moment to pay attention to him.

"What?"

He shook his head. "Nothing. I mean, never mind. But…"

She gestured. "But, but?"

He took a deep breath and blew it out. "Are you gonna tell me what's going on?" He took a step towards her. "C'mon, sit with me. You're not really leaving."

"No?" She grabbed a discarded bra off the floor and stuffed it into the bag on her bed. "This is me, preparing to leave."

Mitch held up his hands. "Okay, I'm sorry, you're serious. But will you at least tell me why? This affects me, too, you know. We're band mates." He took another step. A slow one, afraid that he'd scare her away faster. "And friends. Aren't we? Maybe I'm wrong."

She stared at him. Her purse slid from her shoulder and thumped on the floor. Her face went into her hands. Mitch went to her as she sagged, and eased her to the edge of the bed. He slipped an arm across her shoulders as he sat down beside her.

Damona was crying. She never cried in front of him. He didn't think she had ever cried in front of anyone. That was the impression he always had of her. But here she was, weeping, and it was awkward, because he wasn't sure what to say, though he wanted to help her. It sucked, seeing her this way with no way to fix it.

Maybe it was best that he had no words. The silence did more to help her than anything else would have. She hadn't wanted to cry. She'd been holding on tight to her anger precisely so she wouldn't fall apart. Damn it, she'd already done that right after speaking to Viktor, she didn't need to do it again.

She cried.

Mitch bore witness.

How could he do it? How could Viktor tell her those things, and then tell her that he loved her? How could he admit it after all this time, only to shove her away and tell her those awful things.

"He's dumping us," she rasped, rubbing at her face. "He told me, I know his secret, and he is leaving. I tried to...I offer help, he told me to fuck off."

Mitch was again lost for words. He couldn't imagine Viktor saying that to Damona in anything but jest. He didn't want to make it worse by implying she was making things up, or that her feelings didn't matter, but he couldn't help himself.

"Really? He told you to fuck off?" *When was this?* he wondered.

"Might as well have." She sniffled. "He said he would kill himself."

Mitch's brows knit, and hard. "Huh? Why...I'm lost."

Damona grabbed for something to wipe her face, her nose. She ended up with a knee-high sock. "I know. I'm not connecting dots for you." She blew her nose. "When I saw him, he confessed something is wrong with him, but said if I called anyone to help, he'd kill himself." It was a very short version, but she didn't have the energy to explain it all. Or to speak his secrets aloud. It didn't seem right, no matter what happened, now. "He really meant it, too! I could tell."

She blew her nose again. Noisily.

"Don't ask me his secrets," she said, and looked into Mitch's eyes. "If he wants you to know, he can tell you."

Mitch searched that bloodshot gaze. "It's really bad, isn't it?" He wasn't certain he wanted to know what could be worse than a gutted man standing could.

Damona didn't reply to him, which was a blessing and a curse.

He hated to ask, but had to. He worried about where it would lead. Because he knew she didn't *really* want to leave Viktor behind. She'd rather have a chance to convince him to stay. Wouldn't she?

If he asked the question on his mind then he'd have to tell her he didn't know where Viktor was, and that he'd been worrying about it for at least two hours.

Turned out, she asked first. "Where is he? We missed a gig, eh?"

Mitch looked away. Looked back. Damona gave him a suspicious look in return. She knew his mannerisms too well. She was too observant. There was no point in him playing dumb.

"I don't know," he said. "I saw him leave with some guy, and haven't seen him since."

"Since when?"

"Yesterday." He attempted to rationalize it, just as he had earlier. To himself, outside. "But he's gone off before."

"He never would miss a gig."

Mitch didn't bother to deny it.

A frown creased her features. "That's when I saw him. Yesterday afternoon was it?" She had forgotten. It was a blur of emotion. "Not since."

"Have you heard from him? I mean, texts, anything?"

She shook her head. "He already left. He did, didn't he?"

"We don't know that. Maybe he –"

"He left." An eerie calm settled over her that baffled Mitch. She touched his cheek. "I'm sorry. It's over for me, then."

"But Damona, maybe he's in trouble."

She handed him a sympathetic sort of look. One she might give to a child that still believed in Santa, even though the beard and fat suit were discarded, revealing the fraud beneath.

"Come with me, Mitch. We both know if he's not gone already, he will leave us eventually."

"So dump him first?"

She sighed. "It's not as simple as that. But why not? Save yourself. He's not well."

"You…do you think he's going to hurt us?"

Damona wasn't sure how to answer that. Viktor had warned her off him many times, but never with much detail. Never in the way that he had in his room the last time she'd seen him.

She opted for, "He thinks so. I believed him this time."

Mitch's mouth worked, but didn't bring forth words, not at first. He wasn't expecting her to say that. He wasn't expecting her to run away, either. That's what it felt like; she was running away. But he wouldn't say it to her, in case she bristled.

As he thought on it, he realized it sounded like blaming the victim, anyway. He tried to put himself in her heels. Loving someone who kept you at arm's length, even though you knew they wanted you – and on top of it, that someone was deranged.

He should be ushering her out of the country, not convincing her to stay.

"He loves you, I know he does," Mitch said, feeling desperate, but also thinking the words would help her. "I'm positive. Let's just wait a while longer. If he's in trouble and we abandon him –"

"Yes," she interrupted. "He loves me. He told me. I do not think he's in trouble."

Her jaw set. Her tone had gone ice cold.

Mitch blinked a few times in response. Another thing he hadn't expected. Viktor had finally admitted his feelings, but she didn't seem happy about it.

"Well...so...don't you want some closure?" he asked. "Give him a chance to show up and..." and what? It was beginning to feel like she already had her closure.

Viktor had said it. Viktor was missing. Perhaps it truly was on purpose. He didn't want to believe it. That Vik would just take off, not even a *goodbye* or *fuck you.*

Mitch watched as Damona rose and contrary to the actions of moments before, set about packing. It was methodical. Organized. She even took care in folding her clothing.

Nothing he said after that stopped her, or coaxed another word from her. But he wasn't ready to give up. He resolved to do his best at convincing her sleep on it.

19

Viktor studied Kar over the rim of his fifth cup of coffee. Though the vampire had told him that he didn't mind silence, they had in fact, begun talking. It started slowly, and before Viktor knew it, Kar was sitting across from him at a little round table with two chairs, answering his questions. Telling him stories about himself.

They hadn't begun as stories, but Viktor found that with a little patience, respect and curiosity (all of which were genuine), the Asian began to open up.

Kar had been a Samurai. Though before that, a servant. Half Chinese, half Japanese. A secret his mother had tried to keep, because in those times, the mixture was unacceptable, and could earn one a death sentence in some circles.

Kar was older than his king was, and Michel was nearly 400 years old. Viktor found that intriguing. That Kar would serve someone younger, who, from what he'd surmised thus far, was of a very different background. Viktor considered that this king must be worthy of respect, because the more he was with Kar, the stronger his impressions of the man and his code of honor.

One of the most interesting things Kar had told Viktor, though, had to do with some twins. Young looking boys that were actually rather well aged vampires. Even Kar hadn't met any other vampire twins, nor heard of any. It was possible he'd been among the first to create such, Viktor had said.

Kar had his doubts about that, but agreed he may be in a rare group.

Kar considered them his sons ever since the moment he saved them. They were the same young men Viktor had once played with, on stage, at the *Fall Out*. He remembered them well. One could hardly forget the intense violet eyes, or the white-blond hair. He'd thought them teens, which in a sense they were, and yet…not.

"Why did you do it?" Viktor asked, when Kar explained how he came across them in their home in Amsterdam, over 150 years ago, victims of what appeared a violent robbery. Their parents were dead, but it turned out that Shane and Dane were yet clinging to life.

Kar shook his head. "It surprised even me. I had not thought at that time to sire anyone. I was thirsting, and the house was a beacon, blood scent invading my senses."

He paused to refill Viktor's empty coffee mug.

"When I found them upstairs," he continued, "looking so angelic, it gave me pause." The whisperings of a smile formed. "And then Dane's lashes fluttered. I caught a glimpse of his eyes, which even then were an uncommon color, now intensified. The debate I should have had with myself didn't occur until I'd already spirited both of them away."

This was a good distraction. Viktor hadn't thought once about his predicament while Kar shared details of his life.

"Did you bring them to your home?" he asked. "The one I woke up in?" *Are you in the habit of saving people*, he wanted to ask, but not just yet.

Kar offered him a nod. "I did, and tended to their wounds."

"Like me?" Special tea. He remembered that tea, how warm it felt going down, and not simply because it had been heated. It wasn't that type of warmth.

Kar nodded once again.

"What was the debate you should have had? Was it life or death with them?"

"Actually, they recovered," Kar replied. "I did not turn them until their seventeenth birthday. They were sixteen when I found them." He paused, seeming to consider well his next words. "The issue was what would happen when they were healthy. How would I explain everything? Me, a stranger, having kidnapped them from their home. For truly, I had. They may have seen me as their parents' killer."

It was now Viktor's turn to nod. "I can understand this."

"What happened over the next few months was strange and fascinating to me."

He topped off Viktor's cup yet again.

"I explained what happened to their mother and father. That I had found them and wished only to help them; I had followed an impulse. They listened intently the entire time I spoke." The vampire smiled, which was almost startling. It shifted the mask of neutrality dramatically, and Viktor found himself smiling in return. "I let them alone for a few hours, so they might absorb my tale. They then came to me, informing me that they believed me." Kar gave a soft shake of his head. "How quickly they had adapted. They trusted me. I saw them through their grief, and this was another strange and fascinating thing. It was brief. No mistaking it was deeply felt on their part, but they seemed born with the capacity for understanding that the world changes, things happen, and life goes on."

"Good traits for…immortality, I would think," Viktor said.

"Indeed. They were full of curiosity and enamored of my company. Perhaps some of this can be attributed to their age at the time. Children adapt quickly. But they weren't merely children, either."

He lifted his gaze, which had lowered, and he looked about the room, before looking at Viktor.

"On the night of their seventeenth birthday, I asked them in what way they'd like to celebrate. They looked at me and in unison replied, *for you to keep us forever. Please keep us.*"

He laughed, and the sound was softer and sweeter than any laugh of his before it. "They knew what I was. Or had surmised enough. As you know, I granted their wish, though I had thought to wait at least one more year. But I then worried I'd lose them before it passed. I also realized that they were ready. As you said, well suited, for many reasons."

"When was this?" Viktor sipped at his coffee, rather than a customary gulp.

"Eighteen fifty five is when I found them. I turned them June first, eighteen fifty six."

"Fitting. Gemini."

Kar smiled an even brighter smile. "It rather is, yes. In your astrology."

"It's not really mine, either."

They both laughed a bit.

"Thank you," Viktor said. "I didn't expect so much sharing. You were very forthcoming."

"We're not all in the throes of existential angst, or mysterious and cryptic."

Viktor laughed again, much louder. He hadn't looked for humor from the Asian, either, but that was proving a bad assumption.

Now Viktor couldn't help but ask. "Is this a habit of yours? Rescuing people? You saved them, you saved me."

"Yet you did not ask me to turn you. Though you would not say the word, you knew what I was. Instinct informed you. I believe you've always known. Yet you did not ask…"

Viktor could do little but stare at the vampire across from him for a moment, uncertain if this was more dry humor, or a serious comment.

"Would you have? If I had asked you?" Viktor wasn't planning to ask. He wasn't certain he had the temperament for it. Though being a killer, on the other hand, might make him a good candidate for some vampires.

Kar looked into his eyes, the sensation hypnotic. But the spell was broken when the door opened and Trey walked in, causing Kar to look away.

The lawyer paused by the doorway. "Been up all night?" He winked. "Lame, I know. No brainer." He closed the door and moved towards them.

"Has it been a night?" Viktor cranked his head around, looking for the clock.

Indeed, he had been speaking with Kar all night. In fact, the sun must have risen. But the room was dark and artificially lit. He swung his gaze back around in time to see Trey stopping by his chair. He looked up at him, and could see that he had something to tell him.

"Did you figure out the language?" Viktor asked.

In the meantime, Kar rose, offering his chair to Trey before taking the now empty coffee carafe from the table. "I'll make more coffee." He headed for the door as Trey replied to Viktor, settling down in the vacated seat at the same time.

"Yes. A friend of my friend recognized it," Trey said.

Viktor glanced at Kar just as the vampire exited the room.

"A friend of the king," Viktor said to Trey.

A nod from the other human. "Yes. The king."

Viktor took a breath. "No use dragging it out. As you said, I don't require delicacies. What did you discover? By the look in your eyes, I think it's more than what language I was speaking."

"Or channeling," Trey said. Before Viktor could question the remark, Trey rejoined. "Romanian. You *did* say you knew a word or three, so it wouldn't seem remarkable, except for the fact you were speaking a much older dialect. So I was told."

The Rom's brows furrowed. "Older? How old?"

"According to my source, centuries."

Viktor shook his head. "But…centuries? Has it changed so much?" He couldn't believe his ears.

"I was told that you were using colloquialisms that fell off very long ago. That if you spoke it to a native speaker now, you'd be partially understood, but mostly confusing. It was also your accent."

Viktor needed clarification. Or time to digest. "Because I'm not fluent. I don't possess the accent. I didn't grow up there."

"On the contrary. Your accent was flawless. For a few centuries ago." Trey placed an elbow on the table, and leaned on his hand, studying Viktor in a very intent way.

Viktor had trouble finding words, uncertain what to do with the information. What to ask. The perfect question struck him at last, just as Trey offered.

"I know what you were saying," Trey said.

Viktor gestured for him to go on. "I'm listening."

"You were demanding to know where she was. Who told her that you had died? Where is the one who gave her the missive? Bring him to me or I'll peel your flesh from your bones."

Viktor's eyes widened, his expression something akin to shock, and yet, given the things he'd done, perhaps this wasn't so surprising. Indeed, it appeared further proof of his insanity.

"Things like that, and you were speaking of Elisabetha," Trey said. "Your beautiful Elisabetha, her broken body on the rocks below, in the river."

Viktor found his voice. "That's the name I yelled. I heard that on the tape."

"Do you know anyone by that name, or have you ever?"

Viktor shook his head. "Never."

Trey leaned back in his chair. "No?"

"I swear. No."

"Not that you recall, anyway."

Viktor searched the other man's face. "I *do* lose time. Do you think...do I lose days? Weeks?" Years...

Trey held up a hand. "I have a theory. Given some other things my contacts told me, my theory doesn't seem so far out there."

Viktor leaned forward, curious. He'd never had a sound theory that didn't involve criminal madness. "Well?"

"What do you know about the concept of ancestral memory?"

Viktor paused to consider. "You mean instincts? Genetic memory?"

"No, not precisely the idea that a species' habits may program into a genome. I'm talking about something less accepted and a little more out there...so far. People are researching."

Viktor leaned back. "Please explain, then."

"Well, it's the idea you may have some of your ancestors' memories. That they could be carried in our DNA, with all that other cool stuff. That's the simple version."

Viktor's brows knit and relaxed. "All right. That might explain past life experiences, I'll give you that. But..."

"Would it make you do what you've done?" Trey said. "I don't know. Maybe an extreme case and depending on the ancestor." Trey's gaze became more intent.

Viktor's eyes narrowed. "Why do I have this feeling you've already decided who the ancestor might be?"

Trey smiled a crooked smile, not that he felt the situation was amusing. He thought it intriguing, that Viktor could read him so well.

"I might have a theory," Trey said. But he didn't want to plant too many ideas, lead Viktor into a solution. So he came across as coy, perhaps.

"I know I asked before, but maybe you can answer a general question," he said. "Do you know if you have any familial ties to, oh, Eastern to Central Europe? Which I realize may be a no brainer, but...specific. Be specific."

Viktor arched a brow.

20

Mitch stared down into his empty beer glass. Depressed, confused, and conflicted.

Damona was gone. He had no idea where she was going. Neither did she, from what he could tell. She'd gotten all her things packed, made a couple of phone calls, and a cab had shown up.

Though not before he'd pleaded and pestered and begged some more. She'd responded to every suggestion by telling him to come with her. He'd gotten angry at one point, and flung some horrible words at her. The worst of them were when he accused her of never giving a damn about Viktor, and being a cold-hearted bitch.

He couldn't believe she was going to leave without knowing if Viktor was all right. Or in jail. Or a mental ward. Or if he was ever coming back.

He felt torn, though. He wanted to go with her. He hated that she was going off not into the sunset, but some shadowy, dingy future. He worried about what would become of her. She'd been taking care of herself before they all met. He knew that. She was a survivor. He knew that, too. But they were friends. Friends looked out for each other. And she was vulnerable. He'd seen it. She'd cried.

Angry as he'd gotten, he understood, as much as he could. She'd been hurt. She'd heard something she wanted to hear, but it came with something she didn't want to hear. He still didn't think she wanted to leave, not deep down (unless he was projecting), but it was as if she had to. Like she had no choice, somehow.

He'd felt that way before.

He sat, staring at the suds clinging to his glass, hating himself, and the situation. He'd stayed because he had to know what had become of Viktor. It was wrong to just take off, not even try to find him. It was wrong to let Damona go, too, but it felt more wrong to abandon Viktor.

The fucked up part was that he didn't know how to look for Viktor, or whether he even should. He had no photos. Viktor didn't like having his picture taken. Mitch had one on his phone, but it didn't show his face clearly.

He could ask around, but he was hesitant. What if Viktor had done something horrible…again? What if Viktor was a serial killer? What then?

"I can't do this. I can't be part of…" he shook his head, signaling the bartender. "One more."

He didn't want to accidently bring heat down on his friend. If he were being completely honest with himself, he also rather hoped that someone else would find Viktor and save him from himself and the general populace. If that meant locking him up, maybe it was for the best. Prison in France might not be so bad. He'd heard it was better than many places.

"I'm thinking too hard," he said into his empty glass, just before the bartender replaced it with a full one.

"Pardon?"

Mitch shook his head. "*Rien.*"

The bartender shrugged and moved off.

Thinking too hard. He was a man looking for a friend. That's all. A friend with long dark hair, very tall, intense grey eyes. Bass player.

"I need to find a way to the *Fall Out*. People there might remember him."

Mitch picked up his glass and chugged. After leaving some Euros, he rushed out of the bar, figuring he had enough

money to spare for a cab. If he could just remember how to
get there…

"Well now. How about that?" Trey said, leaning back in his chair. All the while looking Viktor up one side and down the other.

"That's what she said," Viktor replied. "The story she told me. But it had to be a joke. A cute story for a child."

Trey arched a brow at him.

"Oh come on." Viktor's laugh was hollow. "Vlad Tepes? Even if I could trace it, and prove I'm descended from the infamous Impaler…"

Trey leaned forward. "Is it any crazier than the idea of being possessed? Which you didn't seem to think was completely whacked, I might add."

Viktor studied his hands, the table, and then Trey's face. The Aegean blue eyes. "I don't understand, then. If this is connected to an ancestor of mine, and I'm speaking and acting like him," he gathered the words he could, "it still seems that you're saying I'm possessed."

Trey shook his head. "Not by a ghost. By his DNA, if that helps you understand." He held up a hand to stave off Viktor's protest. "I know it's a stretch. It's all a stretch. But I can tell you from experience that possession is real. So why not this?"

Viktor stared and stared at the other man. "You've been possessed?"

The lawyer waved that off for the time being, though he nodded at the same time.

"Consider this, Viktor. Some part of him is with you, maybe, and it's affecting you." Trey said. "I'm not a scientist. I don't know what the mechanics would be, since I haven't studied this. But it's something to look into." What he did not say, is that it would give Viktor something to do. Something to focus on, if nothing else.

Viktor rubbed his face as his thoughts swirled. "You realize if I went to someone – and I'm not even sure who I'd go to, psychiatrist, brain surgeon?" He waved a hand. "I'd sound crazy. Which I'm still not convinced isn't true."

Trey shrugged. "Fair enough."

"It's not like I want to think I'm insane."

Trey shrugged once again. "Okay."

"Okay?"

"Hey," Trey spread his hands, "I'm offering what I can. Another point of view to consider. I'm not lacking sympathy. But I don't really know you, either. Understand?" His brow arched sharply.

Viktor thought that maybe he did. It wasn't about apathy towards a stranger. It was wariness over a stranger who was dangerous, and possibly quite mad.

He went forward with the clinical trial, as it were.

"Certainly what history tells us of Vlad, it might fit," Viktor said, "but how would we even prove it has anything – no." He started over. "How do you *know* it has anything to do with him? When I told you what my mother said, you didn't seem surprised."

Trey leaned on his hand once again, leaning closer over the table towards Viktor.

"I wasn't surprised," he said. "That friend of my friend? He knew Vlad Dracula."

Viktor's eyes widened. Indeed, he'd recently learned that Kar was centuries old. But only *just* learned. Even for someone like him, someone who considered many things possible, it was a lot to take in at once.

"He knew..."

Trey nodded. "I played the recording for him. He's still a bit, uh, old fashioned? He was convinced some devilry – his word – was at work. Sorcery."

"Meaning?"

"He couldn't conceive how I'd managed to have a replication of Vlad's voice, when he'd been dead for centuries."

That sat Viktor back in his chair.

"Yes," Trey said in response to the look on Viktor's face. "You sounded like him. Eerily so, I'd say, judging from this vampire's reaction. And there's the matter of Elisabetha."

Viktor snapped back to the present at the mention of her name. "I know the fables. Supposedly he had a first wife who killed herself."

"Yes, one who leaped to her death upon hearing – falsely – that Vlad was killed," Trey supplied. "That all seems to fit what you were ranting about in your dream state. For lack of better terms. " He hooked his arm around the back of his chair. "For the record, Elisabetha existed; I'm told that was her name, and that she really did leap from that tower to her death."

Viktor sat back yet again. "If..." He breathed in, deep, and out, slowly. "If it's true, how do I stop it? How do I stop doing these horrible things?"

Trey offered a sympathetic look. "Stop being him? I don't know. We need to find someone who specializes in this research, someone who would be open to the –"

"No." Viktor rose from his chair and walked away. "I told you..." He told Damona what he truly intended. He turned to look at Trey. "I will not be locked up, and studied and poked and," his head began to pound, "I can't..."

Trey stood up and walked to him. "Do you want help, or not? Do you want to stop hurting people, or not?"

Viktor let out a sound of emotional agony. "I told you I can't. I end up – Vlad, if it's Vlad – he makes me hurt myself."

Trey's eyes moved over him, and then he proceeded to speak to himself. Aloud.

"Wouldn't that be something if in some way there was awareness? He knows…But that sounds like possession." He paced back and forth. "Maybe it's just that your DNA and his is so entwined that you exhibit very strong traits of his, whether you want to, or not. It's turning into a case of not knowing where he ends, and you begin."

Viktor had no response to that, other than, "I'm aware of some thoughts. Like those. That I'd rather hurt myself, or kill myself, than be a prisoner."

Trey's head snapped up, his gaze found Viktor. "Interesting choice of word. You didn't say it that way before."

"Locked up, prisoner, same thing."

Trey shook his head, moved close, and placed his hands on Viktor's broad shoulders.

"Vlad was held captive in Hungary for ten years," he said.

This sparked something in Viktor's mind. "Captive…secrets…torture…"

"Many say he was treated well," Trey whispered, not wanting to break Viktor's shifted focus.

"Torture, then understanding. Lessons…"

Trey looked hard into Viktor's eyes. Eyes that were glossing.

"Killed my…" Viktor suddenly blinked several times, and refocused on Trey, as if he'd forgotten the other man was there, before.

"Your brother and father," Trey supplied. "Vlad's, I mean. They were killed. Vlad sought revenge much later."

"This is…incredible," Viktor said. "It feels right. It feels like something on the edges of my consciousness. One of my dreams."

"Except I don't think it's a dream, Viktor. It's a memory."

Viktor could only stare at him for several moments.

"You don't think I'm faking. You've not once suggested it," he said.

Trey shook his head. "No. I don't. I dealt with a faker, once. I learned a lesson."

Could it be that he was having someone else's memories? Memories so powerful they caused him to act out, even black out? Was sadism in his blood? His DNA? The idea offered a strange and impossible seeming combination of relief, and terror.

"Maybe you should sit back down," Trey said as he guided Viktor back to a chair.

The Rom hardly noticed. It was all clicking. Pieces of nightmares – memories – were flashing in his mind. Though they were yet more a feeling, than words. Vague pictures partially obscured. The suggestions from Trey, the history, it had triggered something, it had picked a lock, and the door was edging its way open.

Viktor wasn't certain that he wanted to see what was waiting beyond the door. But he had to, and even in his terror, he was vastly curious.

"Perhaps if I study him," he said, "more will come to light."

Trey nodded. "It could help. Maybe I could arrange a meeting with this vampire."

Viktor was still considering other things, and it took him a moment to catch up. "Meet the one who knew him? Would he speak with me?"

Trey glanced at Kar, who had reentered the room on stealth setting several minutes ago. Only the coffee scent had given him away. He yet held the carafe.

"I believe he might," Kar replied, in response to Trey's unspoken query.

Viktor looked from Kar to Trey. "In Paris, then? I'm available whenever he is."

"Ah...not so easy," Trey said. "You'll have to go all the way to him, if he agrees. Bit of a recluse. Old fashioned, too, as I said. In other words, he ain't flying. Don't think he likes cars or trains, either."

Viktor's dark brows knit. "How does he get around, horse?"

Kar and Trey both nodded.

"He's already left Paris, then?" Viktor asked.

"Yes," Trey answered. "We were lucky he happened to be here. Some business with the king. Michel asked him to listen to the recording before he left."

Viktor pondered this, and then gave a firm nod. "Very well. Where do I need to go?"

"Hungary, actually. He still loves his old home."

Viktor's next nod conveyed understanding. "Given what you just said, I should not be surprised."

"I can offer directions," Kar said. "Once he agrees to it, of course. It wouldn't do for you to waste time by setting off, only to be turned away."

Viktor laughed and pushed at his hair. "Wandering is what I do, sir. It would be no waste of time, unless all of my life has been a waste of time."

The lawyer could not help but smile a bit. "Well, then. You have a start. I'll make the calls. Let you know."

Viktor sighed and held out his hand. "It is. However small it may seem to you, it's so much more than I had. Thank you."

Trey looked at the offered hand, took it, and gave it a good shake. "You're welcome."

"Is now a good time for more coffee, then?" Kar asked as he strode towards the humans.

22

The music was loud, the place crowded. *As per usual*, Mitch mused. Not that he was amused. He'd been at the *Fall Out* since the doors had opened, which had been at sunset, hours and hours ago.

Rather, the doors were opened to him by a pale haired youth with crazy violet contacts. Something Mitch noticed was all the rage in some circles. This faddish youngster was hyperactive for a doorman. Hyper for anyone. He didn't look old enough to be working at a bar, but it was France, and what did Mitch know about French laws?

Nothing much.

Not to mention the lad might have been older than Mitch thought. He'd stopped wondering about that when he asked the boy if he'd seen anyone resembling Viktor. He'd gotten hopeful when the so-called doorman knew whom Viktor was. Not only because he'd seen them play at the club, but because he'd played with him briefly, years ago.

As much as that intrigued Mitch, he was more concerned with now, and his hopes had vanished when the lad said he hadn't seen him since their gig a few days ago.

His confidence wavered along with those hopes when the boy warned him – it sounded like a warning no matter how polite the words – not to be a bother to anyone in the club. He was welcome to ask, but not to pester.

As Mitch descended the dark stairwell, he considered that it seemed more a warning to protect himself rather than a case of being kicked out.

Strange warning. For reasons rather elusive to him at that moment, it made him think of the cool blonde Viktor had left with, last time. He hit the edges of the dance floor, conjuring the image of them in his head, in case she was there. He could ask her if she'd seen Viktor since their hook-up.

That is, if he could find anyone specific in the crowd. He was having enough trouble separating people out where they could hear him when he asked questions. Most didn't seem to care, or perhaps it was more that they were so entranced with the music and whatever drugs they were on, they didn't notice he was talking in the first place.

He had some luck when he started dancing with a petite brunette. At first, it was like last time – dancing along with the throng. But the girl started to pay more attention to him, and then to flirt with him. Though he was there for business, he was also a hot-blooded male, and he couldn't help being aroused. This made it easy, her leading him off the dance floor and into a dark corner before he could say *where are we going.*

Her hand was at his crotch, and her lips on his neck, when a jolt that had nothing to do with sex, snapped Mitch to his temporary senses. Though he didn't soon speak to it, the girl noticed that something had changed.

"What is it, lover?" she purred, looking him in the eyes.

"I'm," *what is it with the contacts? Should I get some?* "I was supposed to be looking for my friend. I feel uh, you distracted me and I feel uh…"

Her lips curved into a saucy smile. She squeezed him through his jeans. "You feel good and hard. Guitar players always are." She giggled.

"Um…" Mitch literally shook himself. "Wait, how did you…oh, so did you see us play?"

"Mm hmm." She leaned in to lick his neck.

Mitch was losing his battle with being a good friend. He resolved to do better. To at least get the question out before she got her hand inside his pants and thoughts of Viktor or anyone else flew away completely for a few minutes.

"So hey, beautiful," he said into her ear. "Did you remember the bass player?"

He shivered when she sucked on his earlobe. "Mm hmm."

"Have you…" he cleared his throat. "Have you seen him since then?"

"No. Haven't you?"

Mitch felt a sharp sting by his ear and in reaction shoved her back, without thought. This didn't seem to bother her much.

"Sorry," he said, hand going to his neck. "But what the heck was that?"

"What?"

"Like something stung me, or bit me."

She shrugged. "I don't know about that, but maybe you can tell me something."

Mitch paused in rubbing his neck. "What?"

"Where is *my* friend?"

This was where she made it quite clear that she still had a hand on his hardness, and that she possessed a very firm grip.

Mitch forgot about his neck, due to the growing discomfort between his thighs. "What…friend?" He reached for her hand, but she squeezed harder. This time she gripped his balls. "Hey, damn. Ow…"

"The one who left with the bass player."

Mitch let out a whimper. Her fingers felt like iron. He began to shake his head. The blonde, that blonde, was her friend. He hadn't seen her. He was suddenly quite certain that he didn't want to know what had happened.

"Where?" she growled.

Mitch cried out. His knees buckled, but she held him there. He could only continue to shake his head. Maybe her friend and his friend had met the same fate. Car crash. Thugs. Who knew? He didn't know. He'd come to find Viktor, not have his privates pulverized by a pretty woman. Not in this fashion.

Suddenly, to his great physical and mental relief, she released him. He doubled over, close to going to his knees, since she'd been the only thing holding him up. He didn't see the eye contact she was making with someone behind him. A muscle bound man dressed all in black. He didn't know when she walked away. The first thing to catch his attention, other than the throbbing of his balls, was a different voice. Accented, but not French.

"You be right, mate?"

Mitch opted to nod, as he began to have some sense that this man had saved his genitals from certain doom.

"You sure? Maybe get a drink, yeah?"

Australian. Or so Mitch thought. He nodded and glanced at the man. Bouncer, that's who he was. One of the bouncers. He had some memory of seeing him at the gig.

"Yeah. Good idea. Dunno what her problem was," Mitch said, deciding that to ask about Viktor now might be pushing it. He thought of what the doorman had said. The warning.

"Barracuda, that's her problem, mate. Reckon I don't need to tell you to steer clear from now on." The bouncer laughed, patted Mitch on the back, and walked away.

Mitch watched him as he took a few more soothing breaths. He considered that the best thing might be getting the hell out of the dungeon of a club. But that insistent little voice in his head reminded him that he still had no leads on Viktor, and leads were what he'd come to get. Maybe it served him right, finding his dick in a vice, for straying from that path.

Once recovered, he'd come to rest on one of the slick barstools and yelled for a drink. The Aussie was right. A drink was definitely in order. The bartender was fast, and the vodka was ice cold. He just refrained from pressing the glass to his crotch.

"Seeking someone, are you?"

Mitch turned his head towards the voice at his right. Had the vision next to him not mesmerized him on the spot, he would have questioned why that voice was so clear, when it was so silky and soft. Why he easily understood, when it felt like a whisper.

"Yes," was all that Mitch could say as he looked into eyes more impossible than the doorman's had been. Some very pricey contacts, perhaps. Multi-colored and they pierced the darkness, though he wouldn't have called it a glow.

"I thought so," the golden blond male purred. "You have that look about you."

Mitch opened his mouth to reply, save no words fell out. He couldn't stop staring into those eyes. He felt himself falling, but it wasn't unpleasant. Not the type of fall in one's dreams, where it seems you'll die on a hard surface at the bottom. This promised a soft landing. And other things. Many other things.

The strong jaw line and cheekbones softened with a devastating smile. "What is the phrase? Cat got your tongue?"

The golden man looked away after speaking, gesturing to the bartender, and Mitch blinked. He regained some sense of where he was. His hand flew to the back of his neck. The short hairs there were prickling.

"Not to worry, Mitch," the blond said as he took the wineglass from the bartender. "I'm not thirsting." He sipped from the glass, sipped the dark fluid. "Mm, on the contrary. I always am, for something. But you're safe."

Mitch felt his insides flutter when the man laughed and looked at him. He tore his eyes away. He'd never been into men. But there was no denying that there was something about this guy. Something alluring. Magnetic. Electric.

Scary.

Was that what the French called a *je ne sais quoi*? Somehow, he thought not. This man needed his own phrase. Particularly for the scary part.

"I might be of a mind to help you," the pretty man said.

Mitch wanted to look at him, but didn't want to look at him. He had this feeling he'd never stop looking at him if he started. He could think much easier when he wasn't looking at him.

"Wait. How did you know my name?"

Another laugh followed that made his insides like jelly. "I'm very perceptive. You have just confirmed it for me." He leaned towards the other blond. "But truly, this is my club. You worked for me the other night."

Mitch had to look at him then, and he fell into those eyes. He floundered. Floated. He could not quite swim. Everything after felt like a dream.

"You...the owner? Thanks for the job..."

The man with the piercing starburst eyes smiled. It was a dazzling smile. "But of course. I like the way you handle your instrument. I dabble myself."

"I'd like to hear you, sometime."

"That can be arranged. Where are my manners?" A well-manicured hand drifted to his chest. "I am called Michel."

"Michel..." A dreamy smile attacked Mitch's face.

"*Oui*, Michel. There will be much time for you to hear me play, but for now, would it be Viktor you're seeking?"

Mitch nodded.

"Ah," Michel placed a hand on Mitch's shoulder, and grinned when Mitch shivered. "Most assuredly, I can assist you."

"Okay." A sliver of Mitch tried to shake him awake. It wasn't working. "I'm worried about him. He missed a gig."

"I am aware, *mon cher*. Your Viktor is quite fascinating, I must say." Michel finished his wine, and rose. He held out a hand. "Come with me. I have much to share."

Mitch took his hand, unable to resist. A soft place to land…

23

Viktor stood by the tracks, ticket in one hand, and bag in the other. His bass he'd left for safekeeping with Trey. Trey had agreed on one condition; that Viktor would return for it.

He wasn't certain he'd be returning. While he'd waited for the others to relay messages to the vampire's servants, (*they* favored cell phones over carrier pigeons, much to his relief) he'd discovered that he *wanted* to return. He'd found a new spark of hope.

He simply wasn't convinced that Death wouldn't catch up to him before he could find his way back.

He didn't fear the old vampire he was off to meet. He felt safer going to him for help, to his kind, than he did human doctors. A strange point of view for most, he knew, but he wasn't most people, and humans were capable of horrible things.

It seemed logical to him that a supernatural creature would have more sympathy, belief and understanding, of his predicament. Possible predicament. That such a being would be open to all kinds of possibilities. Trey, a human, had been, but then Trey was special in his own right. He'd heard a bit more about *how* special. And he was, so it appeared, a favorite of these creatures like Kar.

He checked the time on his ticket once again, and again, checked that he was waiting at the proper gate.

He felt calmer. If he were going to die, he preferred it at the hands (or fangs) of the one he was to meet, rather than some lethal injection, or death by experiment. Or prison shank. Because he knew that if he were imprisoned, he'd instigate such a thing.

Why he knew this, he was no longer certain. Did he know because it was part of his DNA? Would this be the response of Vlad Dracula? It didn't seem quite right. Vlad had been a captive for ten years, Trey said.

But flashes of dreams had come back to him again, more than before, and they seemed to link to this time of captivity. There was a sense of empowerment. Of lessons learned.

Some willingly.

It struck him that Vlad was a masochist as well. Something to ask this Julius when he met him.

A train approached the station. His train. He didn't move. There was yet time. The passengers needed to disembark. He'd board after this was over, while he contemplated the journey before him a bit more. A journey he opted to go alone, though he wondered if Kar, his Savior, would have one eye on him, as he'd had since the moment he'd stepped into his life that night in the catacombs.

"Leaving without me?"

Viktor's head snapped around at the sound of that voice and he stared, surprised into wordlessness. Not a thing that often happened with him, but had occurred more increasingly of late.

"I almost didn't make it. Just in time, looks like."

Viktor stared as she looked in the direction of the train, her red hair done up in a simple, high ponytail, and her body clad in sensible travelling clothes. Jeans, some old high tops she refused to ditch though they had holes, and a grey, (because the black had faded) hooded shirt. No make-up and no jewelry.

She was the most beautiful thing he'd ever seen.

"Damona, what are you doing here?" He turned towards her.

She mirrored his movement. "Coming with you, of course."

"But...how did you know where I was?"

She smiled. "Some friends of yours told me."

He didn't know whether to curse or thank them.

"Damona, you can't do this."

A hand went to her hip. "Is free country? I think. I can get on this train if I want to, anyway. I have a ticket. So yes, I can."

He didn't know whether to kiss her, or chase her away. But then, hadn't he already tried to run her off?

"Why?" he asked. Not so simple, that question. But she answered as if it were.

"I love you."

He studied and studied her. The sparkle in her eyes. The determination. He knew that look well. He wasn't going to talk her out of it, he didn't think. It would be for her own good, but Damona never liked things forced on her that way.

"I'm afraid I'll hurt you," he said. More earnestly and frightened than he'd ever sounded before, when he'd said such things to her. "Please, I don't want to hurt you."

This gave her pause. He sounded so vulnerable for that one brief second. Which in turn made her want to help and protect him that much more. She could not abandon him; Mitch had been correct.

She lifted the edge of her shirt, revealing a bit of cold blue steel with a pearl handle.

"I got it covered."

Viktor glanced at the gun and back into her eyes when she lowered her shirt.

"From our friends?" he asked.

She nodded.

"Promise me that you will use it if I even hint at harming you."

She nodded again. "I swear it."

He almost smiled. She meant it. He didn't know if Trey and Kar had explained, or if it was just Damona's will, her love of him, that decided her, but he believed her.

Her hand he could accept being the one to end him. Could she be at peace with it if it came to that?

As if reading his mind, she said, "At least I will know where you are and what happened. That you aren't torn apart by some jackass."

This time, he smiled. Something between them clicked. He didn't question it.

"You do not sleep in my bed, or even in the same room. Deal?" He moved closer.

"Deal." *For the time being*, she thought.

"Where are your drums?" He glanced about.

She moved closer. "With your bass."

"What about Mitch? They said they'd tell him I was alive. I started writing a note…"

"Yes, they say this to me also. He's okay."

He looked down into what he thought were the prettiest eyes he'd ever seen. He couldn't pretend that he hadn't said what he did in the hotel. None of it would wash away, not the bad, not the good.

"Okay, then. If I'm being honest, I'm glad you're here. It's selfish, but I don't want you to leave. So…"

He gazed and gazed into those eyes. He could not send her away. He did not have the will. He did not want to be alone. He'd never wanted that.

Viktor held out his hand…

And she took it.

MEMO

Sorry to do this to you, brother. Our journey is over and I must be onto the next. I know you think I suck for not saying goodbye. You're right, I do. I'm not good at it. It's no excuse, just a fact. I've said it too many times. I wish you luck and ladies, my friend.

Luck and Ladies. What Mitch used to say to Vik.

He looked across the storeroom at nothing in particular, wondering if Damona caught up to Viktor, after all.

"Mitch! Need you back on the floor."

His gaze snapped around to find the Aussie. "Yeah okay. Be right there."

The Aussie disappeared and Mitch folded the note, stuffing it back into his pocket.

He had a smile on his face as he went back to work, because if he knew Damona…

"I'll see you guys around, one day." He nodded, satisfied with that assessment, and headed out to the bar. Tonight, crowd control. Tomorrow – time to play.